Rees I

MW01673715

Celebrities of London and Paris

SALZWASSER
VERLAG

Rees Howell Gronow

Celebrities of London and Paris

Reprint of the original, first published in 1865.

1st Edition 2022 | ISBN: 978-3-75258-792-0

Verlag (Publisher): Salzwasser Verlag GmbH, Zeilweg 44, 60439 Frankfurt, Deutschland
Vertretungsberechtigt (Authorized to represent): E. Roepke, Zeilweg 44, 60439 Frankfurt, Deutschland
Druck (Print): Books on Demand GmbH, In de Tarpen 42, 22848 Norderstedt, Deutschland

CELEBRITIES OF LONDON AND PARIS;

BEING A THIRD SERIES OF

REMINISCENCES AND ANECDOTES

OF

The Camp, the Court, and the Clubs:

CONTAINING A CORRECT ACCOUNT OF

BY

CAPTAIN R. H. GRONOW

With a Frontispiece.

LONDON

1865.

PREFACE.

As in conversational groups one story suggests another, some modest anecdotes may become the parents of a numerous progeny, though the offspring may not all prove equally interesting or amusing, and some may even be born lame; so this THIRD Volume of my "Recollections" is to be attributed to the conversational philoprogenitiveness of friendly gossip. I cannot help fearing, that amongst my numerous anecdotal progeny there may be some abortions; for it often happens that what is interesting or amusing to ourselves from association, fails to amuse others, and I may have noted down reminiscences unworthy of record. But it appears to me, that I am very much in the position of some *raconteur* in society whom a friendly party is bent upon making talk on. The amount of encouragement I have received from the Press and the Public, is far beyond my most flattering anticipations; and in expressing my grateful acknowledgments for the favour shewn to my former "Recollections," I sincerely trust that the present volume will not be found unworthy of a place beside its predecessors.

I hope that no apology is needed for the addition of a few pages dedicated to the famous Coup d'État, which restored tranquillity to the City of Paris, and was the basis of that prosperity and power which Imperial France now enjoys. The public may depend upon the accuracy of the statements I have made, since I have not trusted entirely to my own memory, but have verified every circumstance by contemporary living authority.

R. H. Gronow.

Paris, *August* 1, 1864.

CONTENTS.

CELEBRITIES OF LONDON AND PARIS.

Almack's in 1815.—The personages delineated in the frontispiece are well worthy of notice, both from the position they held in the fashionable world, and from their being represented with great truth and accuracy. On the left, the man with the red face, laughing at Brummell, is Charles, Marquis of Queensberry; the great George himself, the admirable Crichton of the age, comes next, in a *dégagé* attitude, with his fingers in his waistcoat pocket. His neckcloth is inimitable, and must have cost him much time and trouble to arrive at such perfection. He is talking earnestly to the charming Duchess of Rutland, who was a Howard, and mother to the present Duke. The tall man, in a black coat, who is preparing to waltz with Princess Esterhazy, so long ambassadress of Austria in London, is the Comte de

St Antonio, afterwards Duke of Canizzaro. He resided many years in England, was a very handsome man, and a great lady-killer, and married an English heiress, Miss Johnson. The stout gentleman waltzing with the Russian ambassadress, Countess, afterwards Princess Lieven, is Baron Neümann, at that time secretary to the Austrian embassy. He was afterwards minister at Florence, and married a daughter of the Duke of Beaufort's. We next behold, in a wonderful light green coat, black tights, and a crushed hat, the late Sir George Warrender, the famous epicure, whose name was pronounced by Sir Joseph Copley to be really Sir Gorge Provender. The worthy Baronet is talking to the handsome Comte de St Aldegonde, afterwards a general, and at this period aide-de-camp to Louis Philippe, then Duke of Orleans.

The original sketch was given to Brummell by the artist who executed it; and it was highly prized by the king of the dandies. It was purchased at the sale of his effects in Chapel Street by the person who gave it to me.

The Duke of Wellington and the Cavalry.—About three weeks after the battle of Waterloo I received orders from the Horse Guards to join my battalion in London. Two of my brother-officers who had gone over to Paris, Tom Brooke and Hunter, the adjutant, who were to accompany me, requested me to return by way of Brussels, as they were very anxious to see the field of Waterloo. I complied with their request, and acted as their cicerone. On the following day we arrived in Brussels, and dined, a few days afterwards, with General Sir George Cooke, who had commanded our division, and lost an arm. He was still suffering from his wound, and was living at the hotel where supper had been ordered for the Emperor Napoleon, in anticipation of his certain triumph on the 18th.

Sir George observed to us that it was lucky for Lord Uxbridge that the field had been won by us; for had this not been the case, he would have got into an awkward scrape for having engaged the cavalry without orders from the Duke. From what Sir George seemed to think, it was evidently the Duke's intention to keep the cavalry in hand, and perfectly fresh, so that they might have charged the French squadrons when the latter had exhausted themselves in their attacks on our squares. To corroborate this opinion, he told us an anecdote of the war in Spain, which may be interesting, as shewing how opposed the Duke was to the harum-scarum custom of our cavalry officers, who hurled their men at full gallop on the enemy, without supports, and without any actual plan or intimation beyond the ardour of a sportsman going at a five-barred gate.

He stated, when Sir Stapleton Cotton went out to take the command of the cavalry, at his first interview with Lord Wellington, his chief addressed him as follows:—"General Cotton, I am glad to see you in command of the cavalry; and I wish you to bear in mind that cavalry should be always held well in hand; that your men and horses should not be used up in wild and useless charges, but put forward when you are sure that their onset will have a decisive effect. Above all, remember that you had better not engage, as a general rule, unless you see an opportunity of attacking the French with a superior force. In Spain, the Germans, the 14th Light Dragoons, and perhaps the 12th, under Fred. Ponsonby, were the only regiments that knew their duty and did not get into scrapes of every description."

The Duke at Carlton House.—The Duke of Wellington dined frequently with the Prince Regent, who, when he had finished his iced punch and a bottle of sherry, began to be garrulous. The Regent would invariably talk about the battle of Waterloo, and speak of the way in which *he* had charged the French with the Household Brigade: upon one occasion he was so far gone that he had the temerity to tell the Duke he had completely bowled over the French cavalry commanded by Marshal Ney. This was too much for the Duke to swallow, and he said, "I have heard you, sir, say so before; but I did not witness this marvellous charge. Your Royal Highness must know that the French cavalry are the best in Europe."

At this same dinner Sir Watkyns William Wynn asked the illustrious Duke whether he had a good view of the battle of Waterloo, whereupon the Baronet got the following laconic reply, "I generally like to see what I am about."

THE DUKE AND THE AUTHOR.—As everything connected with the Duke of Wellington is received with pleasure by the public, and as what I am going to relate is well known to many of my contemporaries, who have often urged me to put it into print, I am encouraged to relate an anecdote in which I played a prominent part, and which, though it happened forty-five years ago, made so deep an impression on my mind that I can narrate the circumstances as correctly as if they had occurred yesterday.

After leaving the Guards in 1821, I spent some time in Paris, where several of my friends had established themselves, and we all pronounced it to be the most delightful city in the world. I remember Luttrell, at a dinner where several alliterative toasts were given, such as London and Liberty, Edinburgh and Education, giving as his toast, Paris and Pocket-money. That most agreeable of men was seldom wrong in anything that he said; and in those days, as we all possessed plenty of the second ingredient of his "sentiment," we passed a most agreeable time, and perhaps lived "not wisely but too well;" at all events we enjoyed ourselves immensely.

In the midst of this very pleasant existence, I happened to call, one morning, upon the Princess M——, who lived in the Rue Basse du Rempart. No sooner had we shaken hands than she began speaking of the Duke of Wellington, who had arrived for a few days to see the King, and who was then about to leave Paris. She asked me if I was aware that I was no favourite with his Grace, and that he had even spoken of me in no measured terms. I replied that I had not the honour of knowing the Duke personally, and that my position was too humble a one to attract his notice. "You are mistaken," said Madame de M——; "he has doubtless heard very unfavourable reports of your character, for he has warned young Paul Lieven to beware of forming any intimacy with a man addicted to gambling and the society of opera-dancers and actresses, as such an acquaintance might not only lead him astray now, but be very detrimental to his prospects in after-life."

After hearing this agreeable communication, I lost no time in calling on my intimate friend, Captain Hesse, a natural son of the Duke of York's, and who was at that time an officer in the 18th Hussars. I related to my *fidus Achates* what had been told me by the Princess, and asked his advice as to the line of conduct I ought to pursue.

Hesse, who was personally well known to the Duke, offered to call at the English Embassy, where his Grace was staying, and ask for some explanation of so unwarrantable an attack. Unluckily, the great man had left for London, with Lord Fitzroy Somerset, that very morning. Hesse and I, therefore, concocted a letter to the Duke, in which I entreated his Grace to tell me if the lady's report was correct, as it appeared to me incomprehensible that a person of his exalted station should have thus attacked the private character of a man totally unknown to him.

This letter was duly forwarded to London, but did not reach the Duke there; for on his arrival in town he had found an invitation from the Prince Regent to pass some days with him at the Pavilion at Brighton, where my letter was placed in his hands. His Grace, with that promptitude for which he was always so remarkable, replied to me in a letter of four pages. I regret that this document, upon which I always placed a high value, is no longer in my hands. I lent it to Count d'Orsay, who was anxious to have a copy of it; and notwithstanding that a strict scarch has been made, since his death, amongst the papers that he left behind him, in the possession of his sister, the Duchesse de Grammont, I have not been able to recover a document of so much value to me and to society: for it expresses the opinions of a man whose every thought was certain to be respected and well received.

The Duke's letter was complimentary to me individually, and gave a most decided denial of his having uttered any expression that could be considered derogatory to me. He had, he admitted, given some advice to young Count Lieven, but these counsels had no reference to any of his associates. He added that he could not have spoken in such terms of me, as he was totally unacquainted with either my habits or my tastes. To the lady he never could have mentioned my name, as he had not once been in her society during his short visit to Paris. He had never made any observations about the imprudence or follies of gamblers, for in fact some of the best friends he had in the world belonged to that category. He concluded a most dignified letter in his characteristic style, by saying that if I was not fully convinced of his not deserving the imputation that had been cast upon him of abusing me, he was perfectly ready to give me any satisfaction that I might think proper to demand.

I cannot call to mind, even at this distance of time, the noble conduct of the great Duke on this occasion without feeling deeply affected.

Throughout the whole of his eventful career, the Duke of Wellington always placed first and foremost, far above his military and social honours, his position as an English gentleman. How few in his Grace's exalted station would have condescended even to notice such a letter as mine, worded though it was in a most respectful manner, or have deigned to give so full and ample an explanation; and how few would, like the truly great man, have waved their high military rank in a discussion with an obscure subaltern, and declared themselves ready to give him redress *sur le champ*, if he still considered himself injured and aggrieved.

I am proud to think that the great Duke did not bear malice, or think any the worse of me for the explanation I had demanded. In the year 1824, I happened to be walking one morning in the Park, near Apsley House, with my friend Charles, commonly called Cornet Wortley. We had not been there long when we met the Duke, who called Wortley to him, and, after a short conversation, as I stood on one side, I heard him ask Wortley who I was, and on his answering, as I took off my hat the Duke smiled, touched his, and nodded to me most good-naturedly several times.

WELLINGTON'S FIRST CAMPAIGN.—The Duke of Wellington had in his early career lost a considerable sum of money at play, and had been on the point of selling his commission in Dublin, with the view of relieving himself from some debts of honour which he had incurred.

At a dinner party at Mr Greenwood's, of that excellent firm, Cox & Greenwood, I met Sir Harry Calvert, then Adjutant-General, who accompanied the Duke of York as one of his staff in his disastrous campaign in Holland; and he told us the following anecdote :—Lord Camden, the viceroy, had been applied to by Lord Mornington, the brother of Captain Wesley, (so his name was then spelt,) for a Commissionership of Customs, or anything else in the gift of the Lord-Lieutenant of Ireland, as it was the intention of the Captain to sell his commission to pay his debts. Lord Camden, in an interview with Captain Wesley, inquired whether he left the army in disgust, or what motive induced him to relinquish a service in which he was well qualified to distinguish himself. Captain Wesley explained everything that had occurred, upon which the Lord-Lieutenant expressed a wish to be of service to him. "What can I do for you? Point out any plan by which you can be extricated from your present difficulties." The answer was, "I have no alternative but to sell my commission; for I am poor, and unable to pay off my debts of honour." "Remain in the army," said Lord Camden, "and I will assist you in paying off your liabilities." "I should like to study my profession at Angers," replied the young soldier; "for the French are the great masters of the art of war." Lord Camden assented to the proposition, supplied him with the means of living in France, and paid his debts.

Captain Wellesley, availing himself of the generous assistance thus offered, spent a considerable time at the Military School at Angers, where he laboured with intense application, and laid the foundation of that military reputation which placed him above all competitors. It was this education that enabled him to gain his first laurels. On his return to England, he was ordered to join the Duke of York in Flanders, as Major of the 33d Regiment of Foot; and the Colonel and first Major being absent, the command of the regiment devolved upon him. The expedition landed near Furnes in the Netherlands, the crack regiments first; and these, directly they set foot on shore, advanced helter-skelter, fancying themselves on the high-road to Paris.

When the 33d disembarked, Major Wellesley, knowing French tactics, addressed himself to Captain Calvert, the Duke of York's aide-de-camp, pointing out the certainty of a speedy attack of the enemy's cavalry and artillery, and the great probability that every man who had advanced would be cut to pieces. He said, "Pray, allow me to form squares of divisions upon the beach before it is too late." This was done, and almost immediately afterwards, Vandamme, with the whole of his cavalry, supported by artillery, came down, threatening to sweep everything before them. Our troops rapidly dispersing, luckily found the 33d in square, and were thus saved from annihilation. The Duke of York observing this adroit and ready manœuvre on the part of the young Major, called him to his council, and gave him the command of the rear-guard. After continually fighting and retreating for several weeks, the army embarked for England.

The reputation thus gained led to Major Wellesley's appointment in India, where he displayed those abilities which marked him out as the only man to oppose, and finally to conquer, the greatest of modern generals.

The lesson the Duke of Wellington had learnt at the gambling-table, as a young man, was deeply impressed upon him: he never afterwards touched a card; and so firmly did he set his face against gambling, that, in Paris, none of his staff, from Lord Fitzroy Somerset down to Freemantle, was ever to be seen either at Frascati's or the Salon des Etrangers.

The Guards and the Umbrellas.—During the action of the 10th of December 1813, commonly known as that of the Mayor's House, in the neighbourhood of Bayonne, the Grenadier Guards, under the command of Colonel Tynling, occupied an unfinished redoubt on the right of the high-road. The Duke of Wellington happened to pass with Freemantle and Lord A. Hill, on his return to headquarters, having satisfied himself that the fighting was merely a feint on the part of Soult. His Grace on looking around saw, to his surprise, a great many umbrellas, with which the officers protected themselves from the rain that was then falling. Arthur Hill came galloping up to us saying, "Lord Wellington does not approve of the use of umbrellas during the enemy's firing, and will not allow 'the gentlemen's sons'* to make themselves ridiculous in the eyes of the army." Colonel Tynling, a few days afterwards, received a wigging from Lord Wellington for suffering his officers to carry umbrellas in the face of the enemy; his Lordship observing, "The Guards may in uniform, when on duty at St James's, carry them if they please; but in the field it is not only ridiculous but unmilitary."

Colonel Freemantle and the Duke's Quarters.—When the British army was in full retreat from Burgos, Colonel Freemantle was sent by Lord Wellington to look out for comfortable quarters for himself and his staff. Freemantle, after galloping over many miles of desolate country, could only discover a hut. Accordingly a good fire was prepared for the Commander of the Forces, and every preparation made for his reception. After Freemantle had communicated with his Lordship, he lost no time in returning, when, to his surprise, he found the hut occupied by an officer of the line, who, standing with his back turned to the blazing fire, was whistling "for want of thought." The aide-de-camp politely told the officer that the hut had been secured for Lord Wellington, and therefore begged he would

* "They are worthy the name given them by the army, that of gentlemen's sons."

retire. The officer flatly refused, saying he would not give it up to Lord Wellington, or to Old Nick himself. "Well, then, I must use force: the provost-marshal shall be sent for, whose prisoner you will be until a court-martial shall sit for disobedience of orders." The officer surrendered at discretion, and was never more seen at head-quarters.

This anecdote was told to Brummell at White's Club by Freemantle on his return to England, when the beau exclaimed, "If I had been in your place, Freemantle, I should have rung the bell, and desired the servants to kick the fellow down-stairs."

A WORD FOR BROWN BESS.—When the British army invested Bayonne, it fell to my lot to be on outpost duty, and I then and there saw a long shot fired from one of our old muskets which shewed that Brown Bess, though not equalling our modern weapons, had yet some good solid merits of her own, and when held straight was not to be despised even at a long range. Several shots had been fired from the French pickets, when Captain Grant of the 1st Foot Guards, being the senior officer on duty, came to me to inquire the cause of the firing, and desired me to make my way to the front and endeavour to ascertain what had occurred. Having arrived near the ravine which separated us from the French, I stumbled upon an advanced sentry, a German, who was coolly smoking his pipe. I asked him whether the shots that had been heard came from his neighbourhood, upon which he replied in broken English, "Yes, zir, that feelow you see yonder has fired nine times at mine target," (meaning his body,) "but has missed. I hopes you, Capitaine, will let me have one shot at him." The distance between the French picket and ours could not have been less than 400 yards; so, without giving myself time to think, I said, "Yes, you can have one shot at him." He levelled his musket, fired, and killed his man; whereupon, a sergeant and two or three French soldiers who had seen him fall, ran down to the front and removed the body.

A STRANGE RENCONTRE.—On the 10th of November 1813, while the light companies of the Coldstream and 3d Guards were skirmishing in front of Irun, the present Sir Wyndham Anstruther, then an officer in the Coldstream Guards, was severely wounded by a musket-ball just below the knee; and had he not received the most unceasing attention from the surgeon, Mr Rose, he would in all probability have lost his leg. When the army commanded by the Duke of Wellington advanced, in the early part of the spring of 1814, Mr Rose recommended

Mr Anstruther to return to England on sick leave; and he was placed, on his arrival, under the care of the celebrated surgeon, Sir Everard Home, by whose skill he completely recovered, but was not able to join the British army before it had reached Paris after the battle of Waterloo. Mr Anstruther remained several months in Paris, and in the early part of 1816, after dining one day with Mr Boulton, an old friend, who had hired a country-house at St Maur, two leagues beyond Vincennes, was returning to town in a small carriage upon two wheels, called a *coucou*, commonly used in those days, and which travelled at the rate of about five miles an hour. Having placed himself on the front seat outside with the driver, after a time they got into conversation, and thinking, from his appearance, that he looked like an old soldier, Mr Anstruther inquired whether he had served; to which the coachman answered in the affirmative, mentioning the number of his regiment and the battles in which he had taken part; and he added that he was afraid he had killed an English officer in front of Irun, on the banks of the Bidassoa. Mr Anstruther naturally felt surprised at what he had heard, knowing that he was the only officer hit at the time and place specified, so he questioned the driver as to the nature of the ground, and his reasons for being so sure of having killed the officer. The man at once said that about three o'clock on the 10th of November, he and a few comrades ran down from Irun into a small clump of brushwood about half way between the town and the hedges lined by the English; that they had not been there long before they wounded one of the Englishmen, and that an officer sprang forward to the assistance of the wounded soldier, when he, the coachman, fired and hit the officer, who fell, to all appearance, mortally wounded. The driver was perfectly astonished when informed that the English officer he thought he had killed was still alive and sitting by his side. The old soldier even shed (or pretended to shed) tears of joy; and after a minute examination of dates and details, Mr Anstruther presented his quondam enemy with a couple of napoleons to drink his health. This he did, after placing his carriage in the yard of the village inn, and to some purpose, for he got very drunk, to the amusement of the villagers, to whom he recounted his story, and who carried him in triumph upon their shoulders, crying, "Vive l'officier Anglais!"

English and French Soldiers on the Boulevards.—In 1815, during the period when the English Guards were doing garrison-duty in Paris, the usual rendezvous of the soldiers was on the Boulevard du

Temple, where Punch and Judy performed to the great amusement of our brave comrades. It was also the custom at the same period for the discharged officers of the Army of the Loire to congregate there; and I remember witnessing the following incident:—During the performance of Punch, a diminutive, humpbacked man made himself very noisy and troublesome to those in front of him. Two officers, wearing the Cross of the Legion of Honour, were much annoyed at this, and requested the dwarf to keep quiet, and to leave off annoying them. The diminutive gentleman replied by abusing them, and calling them *sacrés Bonapartistes*, an epithet of a disagreeable kind at that period, for it was not safe to be known by that denomination. The taller of the two officers, not relishing the impertinence of the dwarf, took him off the ground, placed him upon his shoulders, and walked up to M. Guignol, saying, "Take back your Punchinello; he has lost himself, (*il s'est égaré entre nos jambes.*)" Our soldiers, who witnessed this practical joke and well-deserved lesson, gave the French officer three cheers. This mark of sympathy from an enemy had its desired effect, for it produced a good feeling ever after, and we became on excellent terms with our former brave antagonists, whom the fortune of war had deprived of their rank and pay, and who were much to be pitied under the species of ostracism to which they were condemned.

"DATE OBOLUM BELISARIO."—The Marquis d'Aligre, the richest and most avaricious man in France, and supposed to be worth three or four millions of money, was once seen entering a church during a charity sermon. He was accosted by a great lady of the Faubourg St Germain, who, holding a bag for charitable contributions, begged him to give her something for the poor. The Marquis did not appear to understand the request, but the lady returned to the charge; upon which the Marquis declined giving anything, stating that he had no money. The lady then placed the bag full of money under the nose of the Marquis, saying, "Help yourself, Monsieur d'Aligre, for this bag contains money for the poor; and as you say you are penniless, pray help yourself." Upon which the old miser, for once heartily ashamed of himself, pulled out of his pocket a purse full of gold, and threw it into the bag.

"HATS OFF."—At a party at the Vicomtesse de Noailles's soon after the Allied Armies had entered Paris, and at which I was present, some of the ladies expressed their surprise that Englishmen of high birth did not take off their hats when bowed to, as was the custom in France and other countries. Dupuytren, the celebrated surgeon, happened to join the party, when some one observed that perhaps the Doctor could solve the riddle, and explain the real cause of such apparent rudeness on the part of the English. Dupuytren, in his coarse and blunt manner, said, "The *teigne*, or scald-head, is a very common disease in Europe; it is therefore more than probable that those foreigners who keep their hats on in the presence of ladies are afflicted with that loathsome complaint." Lady Stafford, afterwards Duchess of Sutherland, who had been quietly sitting on one of the sofas, and whose presence had escaped the notice of Dupuytren, rose, and, in a dignified manner, said, "Doctor, that horrible disease is unknown in my country. My countrymen take off their hats to royalty, to ladies, and to none besides." Whereupon Dupuytren rejoined, "Surely, my lady, there is no law in England which precludes a well-bred gentleman from taking off his hat to his equals, and more especially to females." Lady Stafford retorted with spirit, "You can ridicule my countrymen if you think fit, Doctor; but with all their faults and apparent rudeness, they have never been guilty of cutting off the heads of beautiful and innocent women, as you have done in France." This severe retort on the part of her Ladyship was considered by all present as quite uncalled for; but the Vicomtesse apologised to her friends by saying that Lady Stafford should be pardoned, for she lived in Paris during the Revolution as ambassadress from England, and was a great favourite and friend of Queen Marie-Antoinette. She conveyed to the poor Queen when in prison many little comforts and necessaries; and when the embassy had left Paris, and Marie-Antoinette, after unheard-of barbarities, was guillotined, Lady Stafford regarded her execution as the most atrocious murder, and vowed the utmost detestation and abhorrence, not only of the ruffians who by their bloody deeds dishonoured France, but of the whole French nation.

Hatred of the Prussians by the French Peasantry.—During the memorable retreat of Napoleon from the Rhine to Fontainebleau, the Allies amounted to five times the number of the French. Though greatly outnumbered, yet there was unity of will and of purpose in the councils of Napoleon and his generals, which Schwartzenberg and Blucher failed to infuse into their troops. Wanting neither in alacrity nor in vigour when the glory of his country was concerned, Napoleon, with his handful of men, made supernatural efforts; taking advantage of every good position that presented itself, and attacking the enemy upon several points upon the same day.

Upon one occasion he had completely divided the Allies by his comprehensive and well-arranged operations. Napoleon, to effect this gigantic manœuvre, took the bull by its horns, and accordingly fought the battle of Château-Thierry. In this sanguinary battle the French army succeeded in taking from the Prussians all their cannon and ammunition, and several thousand prisoners. After the battle, General Bélliard, who commanded the advanced posts, naturally took possession of the town of Château-Thierry; and on entering the principal street with his staff, beheld a most shocking and horrible spectacle. The Prussians had committed every sort of cruelty during the period they occupied Château-Thierry prior to the battle, and the inhabitants of that place were driven to such a pitch of exasperation, that when the battle turned in favour of the French, the people acted in a most barbarous and cruel manner towards every Prussian, whether wounded or not, who fell into their hands.

The first thing which General Bélliard saw in entering the town was a group of infuriated women, their hands bathed in blood, brandishing the knives with which they were busily employed in killing the wounded soldiers. The General and his staff had great difficulty in putting a stop to this horrid scene. The women, more like furies than human beings, addressed the General, saying they had undergone horrible treatment from the Germans, who had not only pillaged them of everything they possessed, but had violated all the women, both young and old, and had killed their husbands in cold blood. "Yes, General," cried one of those furies, "I have begun this butchery, and I will end it!" and in his presence she plunged her knife into the heart of a poor prisoner.

Severe Discipline in the Russian Army.—When we were quartered in Paris in 1815, a strange circumstance occurred. It became our duty to provide the guard for the Emperor of Russia, and a dinner was provided for us similar to that which is given at St James's. Prior to dinner being served, our Adjutant informed the Colonel that there were four Russian general officers in our custody. It naturally struck us that something very horrible had occurred to have caused the disgrace of men of such high rank. It fell to the lot of Captain Vernon, son of the late Archbishop of York, to call upon those unfortunate officers to invite them to dinner—an invitation which they cheerfully accepted. During the first course, curiosity seized the gallant Captain; for, in proposing the health of one of our prisoners, he begged the Russian would inform us of the cause of their disgrace. The reply was, the Emperor was not satisfied with the manner in which their men had marched past at the review; whereupon Vernon filled his glass up to the brim, and drank, "Confusion to all tyrants, and—Vive Napoleon!" The Russian generals appeared thunderstruck, and observed, that if they drank the toast proposed it would cost them their heads.

Nothing more was heard of the Russian generals until two days after, when we, (the officers of the guard,) were summoned before the Duke of Wellington, to explain what it all meant. The Duke having heard us, said he hoped that for the future we would abstain from alluding to Bonaparte, for as Louis XVIII. had been proclaimed the King of France, any allusion to the fallen hero would be both impolitic and mischievous; adding that he would make a point of presenting himself at the Emperor of Russia's hotel, and explaining the occurrence.

THE EMPEROR ALEXANDER IN PARIS.—The Emperor Alexander of Russia was fond of telling an anecdote of a circumstance which occurred to himself and the King of Prussia whilst in Paris, in 1815. They had lounged together to the Palais Royal, which in those days was surrounded by a number of narrow streets and alleys, and in returning to the Tuileries, they found that they were in a labyrinth, from which it was difficult to extricate themselves. The Emperor, after a time, accosted a well-dressed man who wore the cross of St Louis, and asked the nearest route to the Tuileries. The answer was, "I am going there myself, and will readily accompany you. Will you do me the honour of informing me whom I am conducting?" The Czar replied, "I am the Emperor of Russia." The gentleman received the information with an incredulous smile. "And who is your companion?" said he. "This is the King of Prussia. But whom am I to thank for this politeness?" The Parisian, thinking that he would be a match for this waggish stranger, replied, "Oh, I am the Emperor of China." Little further conversation passed between them, the Frenchman apparently declining to be further hoaxed. On their arrival at the gate of the Tuileries, however, the *générale* was beat, the soldiers saluted, and hats were taken off, to the amazement of the *soi-disant* monarch of the Celestial Empire, who was now convinced that his companions had higher claims to a throne than he possessed. When the two great personages turned round to thank their "guide, philosopher, and friend," they found that he also had assumed an incognito, and had disappeared.

A Fire-Eater Cowed.—A singular incident occurred at the Café Français in 1816, at the corner of the Rue Laffitte. A celebrated duellist entered and began insulting all the persons who were seated at dinner; he boasted of his courage, and declared his determination to kill a certain M. de F——. A gentleman present, disgusted at such braggart insolence, quietly walked up to this fire-eater, and addressed him thus: "As you are such a dangerous customer, perhaps you will accommodate me, by being punctual at the entrance of the Bois de Boulogne, near the Porte Maillot, at mid-day to-morrow: earlier I cannot get there, but depend upon my arriving in due time with swords and pistols." The duellist began to demur, saying he did not know what right a stranger had to take up the cudgels of M. de F——; to which the gentleman replied, "I have done so because I am anxious to rid society of a dangerous fellow like yourself, and would recommend you before you go to bed to make your will.

I will undertake to order your coffin and pay your funeral expenses." He then gave the waiter a note of 1000 francs, with the injunction that his orders should be executed before eleven the following day. This had the desired effect of intimidating the bully, who left Paris the following day, and never more was heard of or seen in public.

An Insult Rightly Redressed.—Soon after the restoration of the Bourbons, several duels took place for the most frivolous causes. Duels were fought in the daytime, and even by night. The officers of the Swiss Guards were constantly measuring swords with the officers of the old Garde Impériale. Upon one occasion a Frenchman, determined to insult a Swiss officer, who, in the uniform of his regiment, was quietly taking his ice at Tortoni's, addressed him thus: "I would not serve my country for the sake of money, as you do. We Frenchmen think only of honour." To which the other promptly retorted, "You are right; for we both of us serve for what we do not possess." A duel was the consequence; they fought with swords under a lamp in the Rue Taitbout, and the Frenchman was run through the body; but luckily the wound, though dangerous, did not prove fatal.

A Duel between Two Old Friends.—General A. de Girardin, some forty years back, had a serious quarrel with one of his old friends, the Marquis de Briancourt, about a lady. A duel was the consequence. Pistols were chosen; but, prior to exchanging shots, De Girardin's second went (as was the custom) and felt the right side of his friend's antagonist, but found nothing there to indicate the existence of padding, &c. Accordingly, after measurement of the ground, pistols were handed to the combatants. The Marquis changed his pistol from his right into his left hand; both parties fired, and the Marquis fell. The seconds flew to the aid of the wounded man, but, to their astonishment, on opening his waistcoat several sheets of thick paper were found folded over the region of the heart. Notwithstanding this device, the blow from the bullet created a sore on the left side, which was never effectually cured. The Marquis died shortly afterwards.

A Duel between Two Officers in the Life Guards about the year 1821.—A lamentable duel took place in Paris during the Restoration between two officers of the Life Guards, Captain Walsh and Lieutenant Pellew, about a lady. The latter gentleman was shot through the head. It is quite enough to state that Captain Walsh was justified in the steps he had taken, for he had received the greatest injury that one man could inflict on another. Though this unfortunate duel took place above forty years back, I well remember it, for I refused to be the Lieutenant's second, because he had behaved so ill. The impression it made was very great, and the general feeling was in favour of the injured husband.

FAYOT, THE CHAMPION OF THE LEGITIMISTS.—Fayot fought more duels than any man in France. His aim with a pistol was certain; but he was not cruel, and he usually wounded his adversary either in the leg or arm. He was likewise a good swordsman. General Fournier was afraid of Fayot, and only once measured swords with him; while the latter had a horror of Fournier for having killed so many young men belonging to good families. In his rencontre with Fayot, the General was severely wounded in the hand, and ever after Fayot hunted his antagonist from one end of France to the other, determined to put an end to the "assassin," as he was called; but the Revolution of 1830 came, and all was chaos.

Fayot's father was guillotined in the south of France in 1793. His mother, after the severe loss she had sustained in the death of her husband, whom she adored, brought up her son at Avignon, telling him, as he grew up to be a man, to take every opportunity of avenging the death of his father. Upon the restoration of the Bourbons, Fayot came to Paris, where, by his singular manners and dress, he laid himself open to remark and ridicule. In the daytime he was usually dressed in a green coat, white waistcoat and neckcloth, leather pantaloons, and Hessian boots, with his hat on one side. He visited London in 1814, where he bought a tilbury and horse, which he brought to Paris, and in this gig he paraded every day up and down the Boulevards, from the Rue Laffitte to the Place de la Madeleine. His evenings were generally passed either at Tortoni's or Silve's, the respective rendezvous of the Bonapartists and Bourbons. In one or other of these *cafés* Fayot was sure to be found. He publicly gave out that he was ready to measure swords with any one who dared to insinuate anything against the royal family,—a threat sure to bring upon him serious rencontres; but nothing intimidated him. It was reported at the time, and generally believed, that he had, in the short period of two years, fought thirty duels without having been seriously wounded.

Upon one occasion Fayot repaired to the Théâtre

Français to see "Germanicus;" party spirit then ran high, and any allusion complimentary to the fallen Emperor was received by the Bonapartists with applause. Fayot loudly hissed, and a great uproar arose, when Fayot entered the breach by proclaiming himself the champion of Legitimacy. The consequence was that cards flew about the pit; Fayot carefully picked them up, and placed them in his hat. After the play had terminated he repaired to Tortoni's, where he wrote his address upon several pieces of paper, which he distributed all over the Boulevards, stating that he was to be found every morning between the hours of eleven and twelve at the well in the Bois de Boulogne, near Auteuil. Strange to say, after all this row at the theatre, only one antagonist was forthcoming. On the second day, at the hour appointed, a gentleman arrived with his seconds, who found Fayot in his tilbury, ready for the fight. The name of his antagonist was a Monsieur Harispe, the son of the distinguished Basque General. Pistols were chosen, and at the first discharge Fayot shot his adversary in the knee; then, taking off his hat, he left the ground and proceeded to Paris in his tilbury to breakfast at Tortoni's, where a great many persons had congregated to know the result of this terrible duel.

The Revolution of 1830 drove Fayot away from Paris, and he retired to his native Avignon, where he lived much respected by the principal inhabitants of that quaint town. In passing through Avignon some twelve years back I called upon him, and found him much altered, but still dressed in his original costume,—the green coat, white neckcloth, &c.

The Gardes du Corps.—I knew several of those gentlemen who had succeeded in getting into the companies of the Gardes du Corps—St Arnaud, Fouquainville, Odoard, Warrelles, St Roman, Fromasson, and, though last, not least, Warren, an Irishman by birth, but whose father had married a French lady. Warren stood six feet four inches in height, and was an extremely powerful man. He was always in hot water with his comrades, and had fought duels with several of them, and his face and body shewed marks of sabre cuts; indeed, fighting and drinking were his delights. I never saw a man so violent when he had finished his bottle of champagne and a few glasses of brandy: he became quite outrageous. He usually breakfasted, when off duty, at Tortoni's, upon beefsteaks and broiled kidneys; and any one to whom he bore a grudge who entered the room at that moment was sure to be roughly handled.

It happened that Monsieur ——, a distinguished painter, had returned to Paris from England, where he had played a shameful and disgusting part. The painter had been employed by the celebrated Mr Hope of Duchess Street to paint the portrait of his wife, Mrs Hope, afterwards Lady Beresford. When the painting was finished, Mr Hope objected to pay for it, stating that it was a daub. The enraged painter, determined to be revenged, took the portrait home with him, and in a few days returned it with the addition of a beast representing Mr Hope in the presence of his beautiful wife. A trial was the consequence, and the painter was cast in damages. After this untoward event, London proved too hot for the Frenchman, and he returned to Paris, where his imprudence in speaking in no measured terms of the English got him into a scrape which cost him his life.

The painter (unluckily for him) arrived at Tortoni's to breakfast at the moment when Warren was in one of his dangerous fits, and attempted to appease Warren by going up to him and begging him to be more tranquil. This sort of impertinence Warren could not brook, and exclaiming, "You are the blackguard who laughs at the English," he seized hold of the artist, carried him as if he had been a bundle of straw, and held him out of the window. By the interference of those gentlemen present and the crowd below in the street, Warren was persuaded to carry back the terrified painter into the room. A duel was the consequence, in which the combatants were to fight with pistols until one of them was killed: Warren won the first toss, he levelled and fired, and his adversary fell mortally wounded. This duel was much talked of, but no one lamented the result of the duel; for the painter was overbearing, and generally disliked by his countrymen as well as by foreigners.

"I can scarcely look back to those days of duelling without shuddering. If you looked at a man it was enough; for without having given the slightest offence, cards were exchanged, and the odds were that you stood a good chance of being shot, or run through the body, or maimed for life.

The late Marshal Castellane.—Marshal Castellane, a member of a distinguished family, entered the army under Napoleon when First Consul, and was employed during the Russian war. His political feelings were always in favour of legitimacy, and therefore, on the return of the Bourbons, he gladly retained his rank. The following circumstance, which occurred when he was colonel of a crack regiment of hussars, explains the cause of his so rapidly obtaining the rank of general in the royal service:—

A ball was about to be given at the Tuileries, to which the Duchesse de Berri graciously invited the officers of Colonel Castellane's regiment. He, however, resolved that they should not be present, and meeting some opposition to his will, he determined to carry his point by placing them under arrest. The Duchesse de Berri finding that her assembly would thus lose some of its most brilliant guests, went to the King, and requested the royal interference. His Majesty observed to her Royal Highness that Castellane was a great martinet, but that it would be dangerous to interfere with his command; "however, when he comes to the Tuileries send him to me." The Colonel, on making his appearance at the palace, was ushered into the royal presence; and the King thus addressed him, "General Castellane, I am happy to see you." "I beg your Majesty's pardon," replied the gallant officer, "I have no claim to the title by which you have done me the honour to notice me: I am Colonel Castellane." "Sir," said the Monarch, "it gives me great pleasure to be the first to announce your promotion: your commission is already made out. I am certain you will serve me as faithfully and honourably in a higher grade as you have done when your military rank was not so great."

The General was, of course, highly gratified; so

also was the Lieutenant-colonel of his regiment, upon whom, by this advancement, the command necessarily devolved. The first step of the new Colonel was of course to remove the officers from the disagreeable position in which Colonel Castellane had placed them; and they had the gratification of attending the ball at the Tuileries, where, of course, the Duchesse de Berri gave them a welcome reception.

General Castellane shewed himself a gallant soldier, and a determined opponent of mob-rule. Although he did not abandon the service of his country when it was under a republican government, he always boldly proclaimed his preference for legitimacy. When some tumultuous assemblages took place at Rouen, he dispersed them by military force; and upon some of the functionaries of the day observing that he ought to have waited for orders from the government, he unhesitatingly replied, "Had any of the ministers themselves disturbed the public quiet whilst the district is under my command, I should shew them that I know my duty better than they know theirs." He had afterwards the command at Lyons, where he evinced on every occasion firmness and decision. A telegraphic despatch from a private hand announced the death of the Emperor; and he was advised to proclaim Henri the Fifth. A subsequent telegram summoned him to Paris, where he attended the Emperor, who said to him, "Why, General, I learnt that you were a stanch Bourbonist, and that I could place no dependence upon your support." The General answered, "Sire, it is true.I have always advocated the cause of legitimacy; but I have seen that the country submits to your rule and is pleased with it. I have therefore taken the oath of allegiance to you as my sovereign; and I can give my assurance that as long as your majesty lives you will have no soldier more devoted to your service than I am, and shall remain." The General was shortly after elevated to the rank of Marshal in the imperial service, and faithfully and steadily carried out his principles of adhesion to the imperial government.

He died not long since, greatly esteemed by his brethren in arms, and much deplored at Lyons, where he had for some time held the command. There he spent a large sum in constructing a magnificent mausoleum, in which his body now lies. His funeral was gorgeous, as is usual with Marshals of the Empire.

The Comte de Castellane, a near relation, was a very eccentric character, but a great favourite in Paris, where he gave large parties. He fitted up a private theatre, where amateur performances by some of the most fashionable persons collected together the *beau monde.* His loss was severely felt last year by a large number of persons, to whom he was in the constant habit of extending a splendid hospitality.

The late General Gabriel.—Whatever might have been General Gabriel's abilities as a field-officer, as a soldier his bravery was unquestionable. He was the son of a clergyman, and was so handsome that he received the cognomen of "The Angel Gabriel." On entering the army he had to make his way in the service by the force of merit and good fortune alone. Instances of his dashing and headlong courage in the Peninsula caught the eye of one of our celebrated general officers, the Honourable Sir William Stewart, who commanded the division commonly known by the name of "The Fighting Division," and he placed Gabriel upon his staff. Upon one occasion, in the Pyrenees, Sir William was not a little surprised to find that his aide-de-camp was *non est inventus*; and upon asking his nephew, Lord Charles Churchill, what had become of him, he was answered thus:—"Oh, Gabriel having heard the roaring of cannon to our right, has galloped off to enjoy the fun." Sir William Stewart, addressing his staff, said, "Well, then, we cannot do better than follow him;" and off they went. On reaching the pass of Roncesvalles, to their astonishment they saw Gabriel, at the head of a few stragglers whom he had picked up on the way, charge a bridge which the enemy were crossing, and completely rout them. Sir William Stewart was so delighted with this act of daring bravery, that he recommended his young aide-de-camp for promotion, which the Duke of Wellington ratified in one of his earliest despatches to the Duke of York.

Admiral la Susse.—Admiral Baron de la Susse, well known in the best society of London and Paris, was a great favourite of Louis Philippe's. He carried his Majesty to Portsmouth in a French steam-frigate on the occasion of his last visit to our gracious Queen. During the Admiral's stay at Portsmouth, Lord Adolphus Fitzclarence was instructed by the Admiralty to attend upon the French Admiral, and to shew him the dockyard and fortifications. After visiting everything worth seeing, Admiral de la Susse said he was much surprised that our principal port was so badly fortified; adding that an enemy, with a few ships and ten thousand infantry, could easily destroy the fortifications and burn the arsenal. Soon after, the Duke of Wellington happened to meet Lord Adolphus, who mentioned, the particulars of the conversation he had had with the French Admiral; upon which the Duke observed, that if a war were to break out between us and France, and the French fleet were permitted to cross the Channel, Portsmouth would stand but a bad chance. "But the Channel," added his Grace, "is a nasty ditch to cross, and to bring over ten thousand men at one given point; and if the enemy brought fewer, they would fail, and in all probability be taken prisoners."

Admiral de la Susse, in his younger days, was celebrated as a man of fashion. He was rather good-looking, with a neat figure, and was very popular in society. He was in his youth a very good waltzer, and prided himself upon that accomplishment; but being unfortunately extremely short-sighted, he consequently got himself frequently into scrapes. At a ball given by a lady in the Faubourg St Honoré, La Susse, in a turn of the waltz, accidentally, and without the slightest intention of insulting any one, came into violent contact with a looker-on, who, in a German accent, exclaimed aloud, "Quand on est si maladroit, on ne doit pas valzer." Cards were exchanged, and on the following morning the parties met in the Bois de Boulogne. La Susse's adversary won the toss, and took his aim with great coolness, but luckily without effect. La Susse then fired, when the German fell. The seconds hastened to render every assistance in their power; but judge of their astonishment when, instead of finding the German mortally wounded, as they expected, they only found a bullet indented against a well-padded cuirass. La Susse, after looking attentively with his glass in his eye at what was passing, desired his antagonist to rise, as he would have another shot at him; upon which the cuirassed hero rose, and received a well-merited and well-applied kick, without making the slightest resistance, and then walked off the ground as if he had accomplished some wonderful achievement. This extraordinary duel took place in 1816, and was the subject of much conversation for a length of time in the fashionable circles in Paris.

At the commencement of the Crimean war, the Admiral was named commander-in-chief of the French fleet; and when off the Piræus, had gone on shore to pass a few days up the country with some friends, when unexpected orders came for the different vessels under his command to weigh anchor, and to proceed to a new destination immédiately. The Admiral, bent on his amusements, was not to be found for three days; and on this becoming known to the Emperor, he was immediately superseded, and Admiral Parseval Deschenes named in his place.

Poor La Susse never recovered from this dreadful blow, and considered himself ever after as a disgraced and dishonoured man. He lingered on for a few months, and may be said to have died of a broken heart.

Marshal Lobau.—The famous General Mouton, the bravest of the brave, was created Count of Lobau for his heroic conduct in the desperate attack upon the island of that name at the battle of Wagram. His commanding figure and stentorian voice many persons now living may remember, when, as a marshal of France under Louis Philippe, he commanded the National Guard. He was a most excellent man in all the relations of life, but of very parsimonious habits. One of his old comrades related to me the following anecdote of him :—

General Mouton, who was a great favourite with the Emperor Napoleon, was visiting his illustrious chief one morning at the Tuileries, when his Majesty, happening to look out of the window, beheld in the court-yard a very shabby-looking vehicle. "Is that your carriage, Mouton?" asked the Emperor. "Yes, sire." "It is not fitting that one of my bravest generals should go about in a hackney coach." "Sire, I am not a Crœsus, and can't afford a better." The next day Mouton received a cheque on the Bank of France for 300,000 francs, (£12,000.) About a fortnight afterwards, General Mouton again paid a visit to the Tuileries in the same hackney coach. On looking out, the Emperor's countenance clouded over, and he looked greatly displeased as he recognised the obnoxious vehicle. "Did you not receive an order for 300,000 francs?" he inquired of the general. "Yes, sire," replied Mouton, "and I am truly grateful for the gift; but if your Majesty insists upon my spending it, I would rather return the money."

Montrond.—At an evening party at Lady Granville's, at the Embassy in Paris, the whist table was placed in the throne-room. The card party consisted of the ambassador, J. Rothschild, Lamarc, and Montrond. They were playing high points, or stakes, when two ladies approached the table, and in a suppliant manner begged the gentlemen would aid them by giving a small pittance for some poor persons who deserved their charity. Montrond, annoyed at this demand, said, "Que voulez-vous, mesdames?" "Monsieur, nous faisons la quête pour les filles repenties." "Très bien, très bien, madame, si elle sont repenties, je ne donne rien, absolument rien ; mais pour les femmes qui ne sont pas repenties, j'irai moi-même leur porter de l'argent."

Chateaubriand.—This great man passed many years of his life in absolute poverty and distress in London. He was even obliged to wash his own linen. After the restoration of the Bourbons, Louis XVIII. named Chateaubriand his ambassador in England, and during this period his great delight was to enumerate the many shifts he had employed to keep body and soul together ; but what delighted him more than all was to revisit the banks of the Thames, near Chelsea, where he formerly washed his shirts and stockings.

Parson Ambrose.—During the winter of 1816, I had the honour to receive a general invitation to the Sunday Soirées of the Duchess of Orleans, the mother of Louis Philippe. Upon one occasion I remember seeing two celebrated ladies there, Madame de Staël and Madame Recamier. There were many English present also. Among the most remarkable was a gentleman known by the appellation of "Parson Ambrose," a natural son of Lord de Blaquiere's. He was good-looking, and dressed like a gentleman of the old *régime*. He wore black silk breeches, with buckles both to his knees and shoes, and the frills to his shirt were of the finest Malines lace. Sir Charles Stewart, upon entering the saloon, beckoned to the parson, who said, "Well, Sir Charles, I am in a bad state." "What is the matter with you?" "I have a complaint in the chest, your Excellency." "What Doctor have you consulted?" "Lafitte," replied the parson. "I never heard of him except as a banker. Well, what has he done for you?" "Nothing." Sir Charles, now discovering the meaning of the "*chest* complaint," said, in his good-natured way, "Come to the Embassy to-morrow morning, and I will see what can be done to cure your complaint." The parson accordingly went, and found the ambassador at breakfast with the Duke of Wellington. After talking over olden times, when the Duke was merely Captain Wellesley, and lived on intimate terms with the parson in Dublin, his Grace kindly presented Ambrose with a hundred guineas, to take him back to England for change of air; which, he trusted, would contribute to the restoration of his health.

CAPTAIN WILDING.—After our corps d'armée, under the command of Sir John Hope, had crossed the Adour, we were ordered to advance as close as possible under the walls of the town. Accordingly, after suffering considerable loss, we succeeded in investing the town and fortress. The enemy, not contented with firing from the batteries, actually brought a nine-pounder on to the high-road, half-way from their stronghold. This gun did us great injury, and I was witness to a very gallant act of some of the infantry of the German Legion, which effectually stopped any further loss. Captain Wilding, who commanded a company of Hanoverians, suddenly dashed out of a burial-ground to the left of the road, rushed upon the gunners, bayoneted them, and brought the gun in triumph into our lines, amidst the loud cheers of our soldiers. In this gallant exploit Captain Wilding was badly wounded in the leg, and was obliged to return to England for his recovery; but prior to his removal he had the satisfaction to see, in general orders, the approval, by the Commander-in-chief, of his gallant bearing in the capture of the gun. Captain Wilding was a Hanoverian, and brother of Prince Butera, to part of whose vast estates in Sicily he succeeded, and is now known by the title of Prince Radali, which was bestowed upon him by the old King of Naples.

THE CHURCH MILITANT.—I was acquainted, during the Peninsular war, with one of the army chaplains, the Rev. Mr Frith, who was attached to the Fifth Division. He considered it part of his duty to attend the troops into action, and would frequently expose himself, with them, to the hottest fire. He shewed the greatest courage and devotion, and rescued many wounded soldiers on several occasions, performing these, and many other gallant actions, as a matter of course and without any idea of display; for although a man of such remarkable bravery, he was of a quiet and gentle demeanour.

I remember on one occasion being present when a party of staff officers were trying to find a ford for the passage of a deep and rapid stream by a part of the army; most of the horses refused the water, when the reverend gentleman pushed forward, saying, "I daresay my nag will take it," and he was in a few minutes over on the other side and back again. Mr Frith went by the name of "the fighting parson" in his division, and was an admirable and excellent specimen of the Church militant.

Louis XVIII.—Louis XVIII. was famous for his repartees. His Majesty being very infirm, could only shew himself to his people in a carriage; he could not mount a horse, and had great difficulty in walking a few steps. He was very fond of having all the news of Paris, and had numerous visitors during the day, who related to him everything that happened. An ambassador of long-standing, the

Bailli de Ferrette, used to be a frequent attendant at the Tuileries, and upon one occasion the King said to the Bailli, "What news have you for me to-day?" "None worth communicating to your Majesty," said M. de Ferrette, "unless it is that the people in Paris are beginning to murmur because their King is not able to ride and review his soldiers as other sovereigns have done from time immemorial." His Majesty replied, "Oh, I suppose they want a monarch who can ride well. Perhaps I had better abdicate in favour of Franconi."

The Bridge of Jena Saved.—When Blucher was meditating the destruction of the bridge of Jena by blowing it up with powder, one of the old generals of the Empire proceeded to the Tuileries, saw the King, and mentioned what the Prussians intended doing. Louis, enraged, cried out, "What Vandalism! I will place myself on the bridge and be blown up with it, rather than so fine a monument should be destroyed." The King then sent the Duc de Guiche to mention to the Duke of Wellington what had been communicated to him, upon which our illustrious chief ordered his horse and galloping off to the Guards' bivouacs in the Bois de Boulogne, gave directions to Sir P. Maitland to drive the Prussians off the bridge at the point of the bayonet, *coûte que coûte.* The Guards, on approaching the bridge, found the Prussian engineers hard at work undermining; but on discovering we were bent on mischief, and that our firelocks were loaded with ball cartridge,—only five minutes being given them to remove all their pickaxes and other implements,—they quietly marched off, to the great mortification of the officer in command, and to the disgust of Marshal Blucher, who never forgave Wellington for thwarting his purpose.

Louis XVIII. and Sosthènes de la Rochefoucauld.—A few days after the King's arrival in Paris in 1814, Sosthènes de la Rochefoucauld collected together a mob in the Place Vendôme, with the intention of hurling from its pedestal the statue of the Emperor, endeavouring at the same time to pull down the pillar, which all the world has seen and admired. Hundreds of ropes were held by the mob, who pulled away with all their might for several hours; but, night coming on, they were obliged to desist from their fruitless attempts. The King, having been told of this outrageous conduct, sent for Rochefoucauld and asked him whether he had acted in the manner reported of him. The Duke pleaded guilty, upon which the King said, "You are playing the enemy's game; it is by such means I shall be made unpopular. For the future, bear in mind that Louis XVIII. is King of France, and not King of the Vandals."

The Duc de Grammont.—The Duc de Grammont, better known as the Duc de Guiche, was the type and model of the real French gentleman and *grand seigneür* of the olden time. He was the handsomest man at the court of the elder branch of the Bourbons; and during the Empire, when in exile, had served in the English army. I knew him well in Spain, in 1813, when a Captain in the 10th Hussars, and subsequently at Bordeaux, in 1814, when he accompanied the Duc d'Angoulême, and having then left our service, was arrayed in a French uniform as aide-de-camp to the Dauphin. He spoke English perfectly, was quiet in manner, and a most chivalrous, high-minded, and honourable man. His complexion was very dark, with crisp black hair curling close to his small, well-shaped head. His features were regular and somewhat aquiline, his eyes large, dark, and beautiful; and his manner, voice, and smile were considered by the fair sex to be perfectly irresistible.

He served with distinction as a general officer in the Spanish campaign of 1823, and was specially attached to the person of the Dauphin, whom he was obliged to keep in great order. As is often the case with princes, the Dauphin, or Duc d'Angoulême, as he was sometimes called, would frequently emancipate himself, and take liberties with those around him, if permitted to do so. Once, when driving with the Duc de Guiche, the Prince, in his somewhat ape-like manner, pinched his companion. A few moments afterwards, the Duke returned the caress with interest, to the great surprise of the Dauphin, who started and turned angrily round, to meet the winning, placid smile of his friend and mentor.

The Duke was universally beloved and regretted; and I should instance him as being, perhaps, the most perfect gentleman I ever met with in any country.

THE MONTMORENCIES.—At this time, when a lawsuit is about to take place in France respecting the right of a grandson, in the female line, of the late Duke to assume the title of Duke of Montmorency, it may not be uninteresting to call to mind how illustrious a family is about to become extinct in the male line.

The Montmorencies bore the title of first Christian Barons and Premier Barons of France, and have been rendered illustrious by no less than ten constables, and innumerable marshals, generals, cardinals, archbishops, and governors of princes. Their alliances by marriage with the royal family have been frequent; and for ten consecutive centuries, the heads of this great house have shone forth as the most eminent personages in French history, and have held the highest and most important offices in the state.

I remember the late Gaston de Montmorency, Prince de Robecq, a most gallant, amiable, and accomplished man, in whom all the hopes of the family were centred, but who died in the prime of life, a few years after the Revolution of 1830. He used to say that he would never marry, for that the present age was not worthy to possess Montmorencies, now that the age of chivalry was gone, and his country had fallen into the hands of Louis Philippe and the *épiciers* of the Rue St Denis. He kept his promise; and at the present moment, the only male representatives of this illustrious race are the two Princes of Montmorency Luxembourg, both aged men, who have no male descendants.

The name was always a popular one with the French people. The Montmorencies, though proud and haughty to their equals, were kind, generous, and charitable to their inferiors, and were celebrated for the magnificence of their establishments.

Even in the days of "liberty, equality, and fraternity," and at periods of revolutionary excesses, the name of Montmorency has always inspired a certain respect; even the fiercest Republicans have felt a sort of pride when the name of this ancient and illustrious race has been pronounced before them.

In England and, strange to say, in Africa there are still supposed to be living descendants of the earlier chiefs of this family. The ancient Irish sept of Macmorris, or Morris, who have taken the name of Montmorency within the last fifty years, and possess the Irish titles of Mountmorris and Frankfort, claim descent—and, I believe, on well-grounded evidence—from Hervé de Montmorency, in the eleventh century. They have, however, in taking the name, committed a great error in assuming the motto of *Dieu ayde*, which was not the *devise* of their supposed ancestor, but adopted for the first time by one of the Constables of France, a Montmorency who lived several hundred years afterwards.

With regard to Africa, it is well known to all French officers who have been quartered at Oran, that there is in the neighbourhood of that town an Arab tribe which bears the name of "Momoransi," and which is very proud of the family; and the tradition is, that they are the descendants of an illustrious French leader in the First Crusade.

Curiously enough, the Irish and Arab offshoots of the family must have separated from the parent stem at about the same time, and have been fourth or fifth in descent from "Bouchard;" for by that not very harmonious name the patriarch of the Montmorencies was first known. But I much fear that the female ancestress of these Arab chiefs must have gone astray with the pious crusader, and that they are only illegitimate descendants of the Montmorencies; for in all the old chronicles of the time there is not a single instance of a Christian knight having intermarried with an infidel.

This calls to my recollection a story I have heard of a Duke of Montmorency in the reign of Louis XV., who was married to a lady of ancient family and great beauty; but, like many nobles of that time, he was not quite a model of what husbands ought to be, and lived a very riotous and improper life. He even went so far as to appear in public with the celebrated dancer, Mademoiselle Guimard, about whom all the young men of the day were raving. One night, on the Duchess entering her box at the opera with several friends, she beheld, to her horror and amazement, the Duke, her husband, seated at the back of the pit box in which the charming dancer displayed her charms. Whatever might be done in private, in those days a certain decorum was preserved in public, and the appearance of the Duke in Guimard's box was an outrage which the Duchess could not endure. She sent one of the gentlemen who were with her to request her husband's immediate presence, and thus addressed the astonished culprit: "I have always been a devoted and faithful wife; but let me warn you in time. If you ever again commit such an outrage, remember this, that you cannot make Montmorencies without me, and I *can* make them without your assistance." The Duke's pride and fear were roused by this very broad hint; and it is said that he, from that time, reformed, and became ever after *le modèle des pères et des époux.*

OUVRARD, THE FINANCIER.—Before the French Revolution, the largest fortunes in France were possessed by the farmers of the revenue, or *fermiers-généraux.* Their profits were enormous, and their probity was very doubtful. It is related that one evening at Ferney, when the company were telling stories of robbers, they asked their host, Voltaire, for one on the same subject. The great man, taking up his flat candlestick, when about to retire, began, "There was once upon a time a *fermier-général*—I have forgotten the rest."

The prodigality, magnificence, and ostentation of these *Crœsuses* were the subject of every play and every satire; and when the bloody tribunals of 1793 ruled over France, their fortunes were confiscated, and very few of the *fermiers-généraux* escaped the fate which many of them had well deserved.

At that unhappy period, just before the fall of Robespierre, the funds fell to 7, and shortly after his execution and the establishment of the Directory, they rose to 40. By such fluctuations many large fortunes were made by speculators and army contractors; they were protected by the very corrupt chief of the Directory, Barras, and realised enormous sums. The most prominent among the latter was Ouvrard, a man sprung from a very humble origin, but of very great financial capacity. During his long career of success, which lasted from the latter part of the last century till 1830, he made and spent millions of money. He was ruined by making large sales on the funds, under the expectation that the government of Louis Philippe could not stand. He was born in 1770, and his first operation, which consisted in buying up all the paper made in Poitou and Angoumois and retailing it at immense profit to the Paris booksellers, laid the foundation of his fortune. He soon afterwards made a contract for provisioning the Spanish fleet, which had joined the French squadron in 1797, and made a net profit of £600,000. In 1800, he was supposed to possess a fortune of a million and a half of English money. Soon after, he had the contract for supplying the French army in the campaign which closed with the battle of Marengo. His prosperity continued for many years; and, in 1812, the Government owed him, for enormous advances made by him, nearly three millions of English money. He was *munitionnaire-général* for the Waterloo campaign; and, in 1823, contracted to supply the Duc d'Angoulême with everything necessary for the entry of the French army into Spain in 1823, but the non-fulfilment of his contract entailed heavy losses upon him, and in 1830 he was completely ruined.

No man was more reckless in his expenditure, or more magnificent in his manner of living, than Ouvrard. At the time of the Directory, the *fêtes* given by him at Le Raincy were the theme of the whole of Parisian society of that time. At his splendid villa near Rueil, during the Empire, he was in the habit of giving suppers to all the *corps de ballet* of the opera twice a week; and he used to send several carriages, splendidly equipped, to bear away the principal female performers when the performance was over. There an enormous white marble bath, as large as an ordinary-sized saloon, was prepared for such of the ladies as, in the summer, chose to bathe on their arrival. Then a splendid supper was laid out, of which the fair bathers, and many of the pleasure-seekers of the day, partook; and, besides every luxury of the culinary art, prepared by the best cooks in Paris, each lady received a donation of fifty louis, and the one fortunate enough to attract the especial notice of the wealthy host, a large sum of money.

Mademoiselle Georges, the celebrated tragedian of that day, cost him (as he was fond of relating) two millions one hundred thousand francs for a single visit. He had invited her to sup with him at his villa, but the very day she was to come, a note informed him that she was compelled to give up the pleasure of supping with him, as the Emperor Napoleon had given her a rendezvous for the same hour, which she dared not refuse. Ouvrard was furious at this *contretemps*, and (as he said when I heard him tell the story) he could not bear to yield the *pas* to "*le petit Bonaparte*," whom he had known as a young Captain of artillery, too happy to be invited to his house in the days of the Directory.

This feeling, and his pride of wealth, got the better of his prudence, and he sent to Mademoiselle Georges to insist upon her coming to Rueil, adding, as a postscript, that she would find a hundred thousand francs *sous le plis de sa serviette* at supper. This last argument was irresistible, the lady sent an excuse to the Emperor, pleading a sudden indisposition, and was borne rapidly in one of Ouvrard's carriages to his country residence.

The following day the great financier received a summons forthwith to appear at the Tuileries, and was ushered into the Emperor's presence. After walking once or twice up and down the room, the great man turned sharply round on his unwilling guest, and, with his eagle glance riveted on Ouvrard's face, sternly demanded, "Monsieur, how much did you make by your contract for the army at the beginning of the year?" The capitalist knew it was in vain to equivocate, and replied, "Four millions of francs, sire." "Then, sir, you made too much; so pay immediately two millions into the Treasury."

Ouvrard passed several years in prison for a considerable debt owed by him to Séguin, another army contractor; but he lived magnificently even when in prison, and his creditor, strange to say, used frequently to go and dine with him there. I saw

Ouvrard shortly before his death, which took place in 1846.

Madame de Staël.—I frequently met the famous Madame de Staël in Paris during the years 1815 and 1816. She was constantly at Madame Crauford's, in the Rue d'Anjou St Honoré, and at Lady Oxford's, in the Rue de Clichy. She was very kind and affable to all the English, and delighted to find herself once more in sight and smell of the *ruisseau de la* Rue du Bac, which she once said she preferred to all the romantic scenery of Switzerland and Italy. She was a large, masculine-looking woman, rather coarse, and with a thoracic development worthy of a wet nurse. She had very fine arms, which she took every opportunity of displaying, and dark, flashing eyes, beaming with wit and genius.

Her career was a chequered one, and her history is a romance. The only child of the Minister Necker, in troublous times she married the Swedish ambassador at Paris, the Baron de Staël, in 1786. Full of great and noble sentiments, she took up the cause of the unfortunate Louis XVI. and his Queen with generous ardour. She arranged a plan of escape for the King in 1792, and did not fear to present to the revolutionary tribunal, in 1793, a petition in favour of Marie-Antoinette. She remained in Paris during the Directory; and it was under her influence and protection that Talleyrand obtained office in 1796. She was always opposed to Napoleon, and was exiled by him from Paris in 1802. She returned, however, and her presence was tolerated till the appearance of her book "De l'Allemagne," the sentiments and allusions of which were decidedly hostile to the imperial despotism which then oppressed nearly the whole of Europe. The book was seized by the Emperor's police, and Madame de Staël was again exiled, and did not return till 1815 to Paris, where she died in 1817, aged fifty-one.

Admirable as her writings were, her conversation surpassed them. She was "well up" on every subject—"*nihil quod tetigit non ornavit.*" Her *salons* were filled with all the most celebrated persons of her time. The statesmen, men of science, poets, lawyers, soldiers, and divines, who crowded to hear her, were astounded at her eloquence and erudition. Disdain and contempt for her personal charms or mental powers was one of the causes of the hatred she had vowed to the first Napoleon; and, unequal as a contest between the greatest sovereign of the age and a woman would at first sight appear, there is no doubt that, by her writings and her sarcastic sayings, which were echoed from one end of Europe to the other, she did him much injury.

Talleyrand, when he married Madame Grand, a beautiful but illiterate idiot, said he did so to repose himself after the eternally learned and eloquent discourses of Madame de Staël, with whom he had been very intimate. On one occasion, alluding to her masculine intellect and appearance, while she was holding forth at great length, he said, "Elle est homme à parler jusqu'à demain matin." At another time, when he was with her in a boat, and she was talking of courage and devotion, qualities in which the *ci-devant* bishop was notoriously deficient, she put the question, "What would you do if I were to fall into the water?" Looking at her from head to foot, he answered, "Ah, madam, you must be such a good swimmer," ("*vous savez si bien nager.*")

A pretty saying of Madame de Staël's is cited, which shewed her good taste and good feeling. A person in a large company, in beholding her and Madame Récamier,—the most beautiful woman in France, and who prided herself not so much on her personal appearance as on her intellectual gifts,—said, "Here is wit" (pointing to Madame de Staël) "and beauty," (pointing to Madame Récamier.) Madame de Staël answered, "This is the first time I was ever praised for my beauty."

The person in England who was the great object

of Madame de Staël's admiration, and in the praise of whom she was never weary, was Sir James Mackintosh, one of the greatest men of the age, and certainly the best read man of the day. She also lived on most intimate terms with the celebrated orator and publicist, Benjamin Constant; but her *liaison* was supposed to be a Platonic one: indeed, she was secretly married, in 1810, to M. de Rocca, a young officer of hussars, who was wounded in Spain, and who wrote a very interesting account of the Peninsular war.

Madame de Staël was perhaps at times a little overpowering, and totally deficient in those "brilliant flashes of silence" which Sydney Smith once jokingly recommended to Macaulay. In fact, as a Scotchman once said of Johnson, she was "a robust genius, born to grapple with whole libraries, and a tremendous conversationist."

A story is told of the Duke of Marlborough, great-grandfather of the present Duke, which always amused me. The Duke had been for some time a confirmed hypochondriac, and dreaded anything that could in any way ruffle the tranquil monotony of his existence. It is said that he remained for three years without pronouncing a single word, and was entering the fourth year of his silence, when he was told one morning that Madame la Baronne de

Staël, the authoress of "Corinne," was on the point of arriving to pay him a visit. The Duke immediately recovered his speech, and roared out, "Take me away—take me away!" to the utter astonishment of the circle around him, who all declared that nothing but the terror of this literary visitation could have put an end to this long and obstinate monomania.

A Feminine Foible.—During the first Empire, the great ladies of the Faubourg St Germain (like ladies of all times) were very shy of divulging their ages. The Duchess of S——, once beautiful and replete with wit, was congratulating herself on her youthful looks, and pretending that she was born at least twenty years later than she really was, when her daughter, more beautiful than her mother, endeavoured to put a stop to her exaggerations by crying aloud, "O mamma, do leave at least nine months between our ages!"

Mademoiselle le Normand.—One of the most extraordinary persons of my younger days was the celebrated fortune-teller, Mademoiselle le Normand. Her original residence was in the Rue de Tournon, but at the time of which I write she lived in the Rue des St Pères. During the Restoration, the practice of the "black art" was strictly forbidden by the police, and it was almost like entering a besieged citadel to make one's way into her *sanctum sanctorum.*

I was first admitted into a good-sized drawing-room, plainly but comfortably furnished, with books and newspapers lying about, as one sees them at a dentist's. Two or three ladies were already there, who, from their quiet dress and the haste with which they drew down their veils, or got up and looked out of the window, evidently belonged to the upper ten thousand. Each person was summoned by an attendant to the sibyl's boudoir, and remained a considerable time, disappearing by some other exit without returning to the waiting-room. At last I was summoned by the elderly servant to the mysterious chamber, which opened by secret panels in the walls, to prevent any unpleasant surprises by the police. I confess that it was not without a slight feeling of trepidation that I entered the small square room, lighted from above, where sat Mademoiselle le Normand in all her glory.

It was impossible for imagination to conceive a more hideous being. She looked like a monstrous toad, bloated and venomous. She had one wall-eye, but the other was a piercer. She wore a fur cap upon her head, from beneath which she glared out upon her horrified visitors. The walls of the room were covered with huge bats, nailed by their wings to the ceiling, stuffed owls, cabalistic signs, skeletons—in short, everything that was likely to impress a weak or superstitious mind. This malignant-looking Hecate had spread out before her several packs of cards, with all kinds of strange figures and ciphers depicted on them. Her first question, uttered in a deep voice, was whether you would have the *grand* or *petit jeu*, which was merely a matter of form. She then inquired your age, and what was the colour and the animal you preferred. Then came, in an authoritative voice, the word "*Coupez*," repeated at intervals, till the requisite number of cards from the various packs were selected and placed in rows side by side. No further questions were asked, and no attempt was made to discover who or what you were, or to watch upon your countenance the effect of the revelations. She neither prophesied smooth things to you nor tried to excite your fears, but seemed really to believe in her own power. She informed me that I was *un militaire*, that I should be twice married and have several children, and foretold many other events which have also come to pass, though I did not at the time believe one word of the sibyl's prediction.

Mademoiselle le Normand was born in 1768, and was already celebrated as a fortune-teller so early as 1790. She is said to have predicted to the unfortunate Princesse de Lamballe her miserable death at the hands of the infuriated populace. She is also reported to have been frequently visited and consulted by Robespierre and St Just; to have reported his downfall to Danton, at that time the idol of the people; to have warned the famous General Hoche of his approaching death by poison; to have foretold to Bernadotte a northern throne, and to Moreau exile and an untimely grave.

The Empress Josephine, who, like most creoles, was very superstitious, used frequently to send for Mademoiselle le Normand to the Tuileries, and put great faith in her predictions; which she always asserted in after years had constantly been verified. But, unfortunately for the sibyl, she did not content herself with telling Josephine's fortune, but actually ventured to predict a future replete with malignant influences to the Emperor himself. This rash conduct entailed upon her great misfortunes and a long imprisonment; but she survived all her troubles, and died as late as 1843, having long before given up fortune-telling, by which she had amassed a large sum of money.

An Ominous Fall.—I remember Count d'Orsay telling me that on the day previous to the appearance of the celebrated *ordonnances,* or decrees of July 27, 1830, which caused the Revolution and drove Charles X. from the throne, his sister, the Duchesse de G——, niece by marriage to Prince Polignac, and a violent Royalist, was seated at the piano, playing and singing with triumphant vigour, "*La victoire est à nous,*" when suddenly the music-stool gave way, and the beautiful Duchess lay sprawling on the floor. D'Orsay, who was a Liberal, assured her, laughingly, that this fall in the midst of her Legitimist song was *de très mauvais augure,* and a bad prognostic for the success of the party to which she belonged. He did not at the time believe his own prophecy, so firmly did the Bourbons appear to be established; but before the end of the month Charles X. had left France, and was followed by the fair Duchess and her husband, the most faithful friends and adherents of the fallen monarch, and as true to him in adversity as when he shone forth as one of the most powerful sovereigns of Europe.

Louis Philippe and Marshal Soult.—Louis Philippe's cunning was proverbial, and he shewed great talent and ingenuity in managing his ministers; but he had great difficulties to encounter. The most *exigeant* of all his officials was the celebrated Marshal Soult, who was perpetually asking the King for some place or appointment for one or other of his friends or relations, to the disgust of Louis Philippe. Upon one occasion, when all the ministers had assembled in the royal closet, the King, observing that the Marshal appeared displeased, inquired, "What is the matter, Marshal?" "Oh, nothing, sire; except that I intend giving into your Majesty's hands my resignation." This untoward and unexpected announcement alarmed the rest of the ministers, who, one and all, intimated that in such case they also must tender their resignations. The King, not alarmed in the slightest degree, requested the Marshal would follow him into his private room, and begged the rest of the ministers to remain until his return. The interview lasted a considerable time, and the King, fearing that he had kept the ministers too long waiting, and that their patience was exhausted, popped his head into the council-room, crying out, "A little more patience, gentlemen. All will be well; for the Marshal and myself have already shed tears." The truth became known the following day; at all events it was generally whispered that Soult had frightened the King out of a promise that all places of emolument and advancement in the army should centre in him, which promise was religiously adhered to until Soult left the ministry of war.

Decamps and the Duke of Orleans.—Some twenty years back, or thereabout, I was breakfasting with my late lamented friend, Lord H. Seymour, when Decamps, the celebrated painter, was announced. During breakfast Decamps told us the following anecdote, which, he said, had occurred the day before :—A gentleman called at his lodging, on the third story, and asked the porter if M. Decamps was at home, and being answered in the affirmative, the visitor was about to ascend the staircase when the porter called after him, and said, "As you are about to visit the artist, perhaps you will have no objection to carry with you his trousers, which I have just mended." "By all means," replied the stranger; "I shall be happy to render you this little service." Arriving at the door, the visitor rang the bell, and Decamps, on opening the door, to his utter amazement, recognised the Duke of Orleans, who laughingly presented to him the trousers he had received from the porter. This little anecdote is one out of many I could relate to illustrate the truly amiable character and unaffected simplicity of the lamented heir of Louis Philippe's throne.

FASHION IN PARIS.—It has been said of the French that they are constant only in their fickleness, worshipping one day what they execrate the next, and throwing down with their own hands from its pedestal the idol they themselves had set up a few weeks before. But there is one deity to whom they have never proved faithless; at whose shrine they bow with the same devotion to-day as they did centuries ago, whose fiat is law, and whose dictates none dare resist. This capricious, exacting, ever-changing goddess is Fashion.

I remember once expressing my admiration for a very handsome, charming lady, in the presence of a Parisian "man-milliner of modern days." During all my encomiums the Gaul preserved a stern silence. "Do you not admire Lady X——?" I asked, rather provoked by his disdainful looks. "She has purple gloves—c'est une femme jugée," he replied, with a look of supreme contempt, which was truly amusing to behold. Though it is now the fashion in Paris to imitate the fast generation of perfidious Albion in many articles of dress, such as looped-up petticoats, wideawake hats, nets for the hair, and Balmoral boots, in former days no English lady who had not been brought up at the feet of some female Parisian Gamaliel, could be supposed by any possibility to know anything about *la toilette*.

Many years ago I was asked one day to dine with the late Lord Pembroke, to meet Lord C——, and a goodly array of French *élégants.* Even after this lapse of years I can still smile at the recollection of the anxiety with which these gentlemen —among whom, by the by, was the handsome Henri de Noailles, afterwards Duc de Mouchy—awaited the arrival of the celebrated London dandy. At length the great man was announced; for, true to London rule, he came last, and long after the hour fixed for dinner. There was no one more agreeable or cleverer than Lord C——, and no one, at the time of which I write, was more the fashion in London; but to appreciate him one required to be accustomed to his peculiar appearance and rather eccentric manner. Short of stature, and rather inclined to be obese, even at five-and-twenty, he wore a coat very much thrown open, a variety of splendid jewels adorning a transparent cambric shirt elaborately embroidered, and (oh, tell it not in Gath!) an exceedingly short, rose-coloured waistcoat, just covering his ample chest, and cutting his somewhat square-built torso exactly in two. Add to this, very long, straight, straw-coloured hair, which he had the habit of throwing continually back, or, by a rapid gesture, bringing forward to fall over his wild but very expressive eyes, and his *tout ensemble* appeared, to French notions, very strange indeed: the Parisian exquisites could hardly believe that they saw before them the Lovelace, the *fleur des pois* of English society, of whom they had heard so much.

Those who, like myself, are old enough to recollect the beautiful Lady Blessington in her brightest days, can remember that she always wore a peculiar costume, chosen with artistic taste to suit exactly her style of beauty. The cap she was in the habit of wearing has been drawn in Chalon's portrait of her, well known from the print in the "Keepsake," and in all the shop windows of the day. It was "a mob-cap" behind, drawn in a straight line over the forehead, where, after a slight fulness on each temple, giving it a little the appearance of wings, it was drawn down close over the cheeks, and fastened under the chin. Nothing could have been more cunningly devised to shew off the fine brow and beautifully-shaped oval face of the deviser, or to conceal the too great width of the cheeks, and a premature development of double chin. Lady Blessington had also a style of dress suitable to her figure, which was full, but then not "of o'er-grown bulk." She always wore white in the morning, a thick muslin dress, embroidered in front and lined with some bright colour, and a large silk bonnet and cloak to match. This was her costume in London, but, on her arrival in Paris, two or three French ladies got hold of her, declared she was *horriblement fagotée,* and insisted on having her dressed in quite a different style by a fashionable *modiste;* they managed so completely to transform her that, in the opinion of myself and all who had seen her in England, her defects were brought out, and all her beauty disappeared. But, nevertheless, in her new and unbecoming attire, she was pronounced *charmante* by a jury of fashionable dames, and forced, *nolens volens,* to take an eternal farewell to the lovely and becoming costumes of her youth.

Fashion has such a wonderful power over the French mind, that it can actually transform the body so as to suit the exigency of the moment. In former days, we old fellows may remember that the French type of womankind was *une petite femme mignonne et brune.* In the whole of society, thirty or forty years ago, one could scarcely have numbered more than half-a-dozen tall women. They were looked upon as anomalies, and saluted not unfrequently with such very uncomplimentary appellations as "*chameaux gensdarmes,*" "*asperges,*" &c., &c. Now that it is the fashion to be tall and commanding, one sees dozens of gigantic women every day that one goes out, with heels inside as well as outside their boots; perhaps even stilts under those long sweeping petticoats. I know not how the change has been effected, but there it is.

Frenchwomen used to have dark hair; blondes were not generally admired, and tried by every possible means to darken their hair; but now, since the Empress has made fair hair *à la mode,* all the women must be blondes, and what with gold powder and light wigs they *do* succeed. As to complexions, a dark one is now unknown; roses and lilies abound on every cheek: even some young men of fashion have not disdained the use of cosmetics, but have come out from the hands of the *coiffeur* romantically pale or delicately tinted.

Fashion is very capricious, and it does not suffice to sit in high places in order to govern *la mode.* With the exception of the Duke of Orleans, so prematurely cut off in the flower of his youth, not one of Louis Philippe's family, male or female, ever exercised the smallest influence over this capricious goddess. There were young and handsome princesses, always well and tastefully dressed, but they were pronounced *rococo;* and no one ever dreamt of wearing any particular bonnet or cloak, because the beautiful Duchesse de Nemours, or the graceful Princesse de Joinville had appeared in a similar one.

It is not because the Empress Eugènie is the wife of Napoleon III. that she sets the fashion, even to those who don't go to court, and who turn up their noses at her *entourage.* She is considerably older and certainly not handsomer than was the Duchesse de Nemours, when she left France to die in exile; but she has the *chic,* if I may use such a word, that the Orleans princesses did not possess; and the quietest dowager, before she ventures to adopt a *coiffure,* as well as the gayest lady of the *demi-monde,* will cast a look to see what the Empress wears. Strange to say, the supreme good taste and elegance which reign in her Majesty's *toilettes* were by no means conspicuous in her younger days; for, as Mademoiselle Montijo, she was voted beautiful and charming, but very ill-dressed.

The style of French cookery has also changed as completely as the style of dress, at the dictates of Fashion. Modern attire and modern cookery are alike over ornamented. Thirty years ago, simplicity in dress, especially in the morning, was the right thing: if by any extraordinary chance a Parisian lady of rank condescended to take a walk, (a rare occurrence,) she could only be remarked by the extreme plainness and neatness of her attire; and any article of dress that could in anywise resemble what might be worn by the *lorette* of that day was studiously shunned. To be taken for anything of a lower grade than what she was, and spoken to by an unknown person, would have been looked on as an insult so great that the humiliating incident would never have been breathed to mortal ear; but now-a-days it is considered only a good joke. How astonished and horror-struck would be the great ladies of the Restoration, if they could rise from their graves and behold their granddaughters emulating the *demi-monde* in their dress, language, and manners; *affichant* their *liaisons* in the sight of the sun; walking into their lovers' houses unveiled, undisguised, or riding with them publicly, and having their carriages called under their own names at the restaurants, or small theatres, where they have been *tête-à-tête!*

The dignified, artful, proud, but perhaps not more virtuous, grandmother would have been unutterably disgusted, not so much at the immorality as at the bad taste displayed in such arrangements; which then existed just as much as now, but were supposed to be unknown. Great was the amusement of the clever and charming Lady G——, at one of her small receptions thirty years ago, at seeing the celebrated statesman, Comte M——, saluting in the most respectful and distant manner, and with all the formal politeness of *la vieille cour*, the Comtesse de C——, with whom it was supposed that he had long been on terms of more than friendly intimacy, and whom he had probably left but a few hours before. The lady, without even extending the "shake hands" now so much in vogue, returned the salutation by an equally reserved and dignified courtesy; and a minute after this formal greeting, Lady G—— overheard the elderly minister, in a voice full of enthusiastic admiration, address the middle-aged lady thus, "Pauline, tu as 15 ans!"

I am sorry to say that *esclandres*, or scandals which made a noise in the world, were supposed to be perpetrated by my countrywomen alone. Comte Alfred de Maussion, a very dark, handsome man, who was a great Lovelace, especially amongst the English ladies some forty years ago, used to say, "Those charming Englishwomen are really *très compromettantes.* They are not happy if they do not run away from their stupid, good-natured husbands, who only ask to be permitted to shut their eyes and see nothing."

Certainly in these modern times the order of things is reversed. Frenchmen need not take the trouble of publishing their successes with their own countrywomen; their victims are only too happy to relate them: indeed, modern French husbands would consider their wives very *rococo* and *provinciales*, if they had not at least one *cicisbeo* to follow in their train. *Le mari trompé* exists now only in the drama or novel. His eyes are wide open; no one tries to deceive him; and he is perfectly satisfied.

Literary Salons in France.—One of the most agreeable *salons* in Paris was held by the late Madame Emile de Girardin, the Mrs Norton of France. Like our own gifted countrywoman, she was endowed not only with poetic genius, but likewise with great conversational wit and much personal beauty.

She was a tall, good-looking woman, with the aspect of a Muse, or rather of what one fancies a Muse ought to be. She had an abundance of beautiful fair hair, large blue eyes, an aquiline nose, and very fine teeth, and bore a striking resemblance to the pictures of Marie-Antoinette. She was also somewhat like the beautiful Duchesse de Guiche, (mother of the French ambassador at Vienna;) but it was remarked that she looked like the case in which Madame de Guiche had been laid, being of coarser build, and with larger features; though in intellectual gifts Madame de Girardin was considerably the other lady's superior.

"She had many great and estimable qualities. Her mind and heart, like her outward frame, were on a large and grand scale. She was above all the littlenesses that too often disfigure women's characters. She was (a rare thing in a woman) an enthusiastic admirer of beauty even in her own sex, and took pleasure in drawing round her the women most distinguished for their personal or mental qualities. She possessed a peculiar knack of making her guests appear to the best advantage, drawing them out, and placing them in the little circle where they would be sure to shine and be appreciated; for she felt that she could afford to subdue the light of her brilliant wit, and allow the little glowworms around her to twinkle to their own satisfaction.

You were sure to meet in the *salon* of Madame E. de Girardin all the celebrities of the day, whether fashionable, literary, or political—Lamartine, Balzac, Dumas, Fredcric Soulié, Emile Souvestre, Theophile Gautier, with the Dukes and Counts of the Faubourg St Germain, Orleanist deputies, and the handsome Englishwomen who used to gladden Parisian eyes and win Parisian hearts.

Every one felt at ease,—the women looked their best, the men made themselves agreeable, and the charming hostess seemed happy in the enjoyment of those around her.

Any one who wishes in some degree to appreciate the brilliant and vivacious wit of Madame E. de Girardin may obtain some idea of it by reading the charming "Lettres Parisiennes," published under the pseudonyme of Vicomtesse de Launay; though (admirable as they are) they give only a dim reflection of that true *esprit Français,* which Madame de Girardin possessed in its highest perfection, and the great charm of which lies in quick repartees and the *à propos* of the moment.

In addition to her great gifts as a prose writer, she was also a poetess of the highest order; and her *pièces de théâtre* enjoyed the greatest popularity, and met with well-deserved success.

Though in reality far superior to her husband, both in cleverness and judgment, she had a high and even exaggerated opinion of his merits as a politician. In the darkest days of that melancholy experiment yclept the *République Française* of 1848, an intimate friend was sitting one morning in Madame de Girardin's boudoir. They were lamenting over the miserable state of things which had succeeded the era of constitutional liberty. After discussing the dangers and difficulties of the moment, Madame de Girardin added, with a grave expression of countenance, and a deeper intonation of voice, "Happily, there is one above who can restore order and tranquillity to the country; and he alone can save us." The visitor, somewhat astonished at what he thought a pious observation coming from a lady of rather Voltairian principles, muttered out something about Providence, and good coming out of evil. "That 's not the question," said Madame de Girardin; "I am not talking about Providence, but of my husband, who is at this moment overhead, and engaged in writing an article for the *Presse*, which will appear to-morrow, and set everything to rights."

Madame de Girardin and her sister, Madame O'Donnell, a very clever and agreeable, but less good-natured woman, both inherited their great gifts from their mother, Madame Sophie Gay, the celebrated authoress of "Les Malheurs d'un Amant Heureux," and other novels, much appreciated some thirty or forty years ago.

Salons like that of the gifted Madame Emile de Girardin are extremely rare now-a-days, owing greatly to the unlimited extension of what is called society; and also, perhaps, in some measure, to the strong line of demarcation drawn by political animosity. The thirst for noisy active pleasure has well-nigh destroyed the charming little *coteries* of the olden time, where men did not think it beneath them to be well-bred and amiable, where they consented to speak of other things besides their horses and mistresses, and where women were not satisfied with being pretty and well-dressed, but aimed also at being thought clever and agreeable.

One of the pleasantest of these *salons* was that of the Comtesse Merlin. In a different way, that lady was almost as remarkable a person as Madame Emile de Girardin. She was a Spanish Creole by birth ; and though even when I made her acquaintance, some thirty years ago, she was what our English novelists call "somewhat *embonpoint*," her beauty was still of the very highest order. Her face was one which, once beheld, could never be forgotten ; the perfect oval of the contour, the small regular features, fine brow, and dark flashing eyes were in perfect harmony. Though she had the Spanish defect of a too long *corsage*, and a somewhat thick waist, yet her bust and arms were faultless.

And she was not only surpassingly beautiful, but possessed a voice equal to those of any of the first-rate singers who have appeared upon the stage. She could sing with Malibran, Grisi, Rubini, and Tamburini, without appearing out of place. In her latter years what once had been so great a charm became the terror of her friends ; for she did not feel her declining powers, and her voice, which had become uncertain, and even hoarse, sounded in her own ears as mellow and enchanting as ever. She was one of those who will not grow old. As she approached sixty, her gowns became more *décolletées,* and her bravuras more frequent. She used to have all her gray hairs plucked out ; so that at last, as was wittily observed, instead of being *coiffée en cheveux,* she was *coiffée en tête.*

But perhaps these illusions as to her appearance and perpetual youth enabled Madame Merlin up to the end of her life to remain the same kind, generous-hearted, agreeable woman she had been in her young days, when all the world was at her feet. She still thought herself far superior to the young beauties who had succeeded her ; and no doubt even the sear and yellow leaf of her autumnal time was more attractive than the spring of many younger ones around her.

She had less wit and more genuine good-nature than Madame de Girardin. She might have a moment of violent anger, but bore no malice ; and she had too much reliance on the variety of her attractions to fear any rivalry. As the *étudiant* says in the well-known print of Gavarni, "*C'était là une riche nature de femme, et si bon enfant.*"

Madame Merlin gave charming concerts, followed

by very agreeable suppers. Her house was a sort of neutral ground, where the ministers of the Orleans dynasty met the leaders of the Legitimist party, and the most celebrated writers of the day; where Duchesses sat down with singers, and all aristocratic pretensions were laid aside. Madame Merlin, among her many good qualities, had one which is rare and admirable, and is the stamp of a truly noble nature. She was thoroughly independent. The poor way-worn musician who formed one of a chorus met with as civil and kind a reception as the Duke or Count just arrived from the Faubourg St Germain. There was the kind, beaming, southern smile of recognition for the second-rate artiste, when met in some great house where he or she was kept at arm's length. There was in her no respect of persons for their rank or position, no cringing to the debasing laws of social etiquette. She possessed what is much rarer than we all imagine,—a truly kind heart; and she reaped her reward, for though Madame Merlin had not always a great regard for appearances, no one had the courage to fling a stone at the generous-minded, warm-hearted woman.

Sir John Elley.—I have alluded in my former volume to the extraordinary personal bravery of

General Sir John Elley on the field of Waterloo, and his series of hand-to-hand encounters with the French cavalry on that great day. It is perhaps not generally known that this most distinguished officer commenced his career as a private in the Blues. He afterwards commanded that celebrated regiment, for which he always had a great liking; and on a lengthened tour he once made through Europe, after the war, although a Major-general, he always wore the uniform of the Royal Horse Guards.

When he arrived at Vienna, he was invited to dine at a full-dress dinner at the British Ambassador's, on the occasion of King George IV.'s birthday. He was covered with orders, bestowed by the different sovereigns of Europe in 1815; and amongst these gorgeous ribands and crosses the modest Waterloo medal appeared. Sir John happened to sit next to a French Secretary of Embassy, who criticised the English decoration, and said, "Surely, General, that is a very poor sort of order the Government have given you and the other brave officers of the English army. It cannot have cost them five francs." "True," replied Sir John, making a low bow, "it has not cost our country more than five francs; but it cost yours a Napoleon."

An English Dandy in Paris.—During the days of Georges III. and IV., a number of gentlemen, remarkable for their eccentricities of dress and manners, were the lions of the day both in London and Paris. For example, we had such men as Brummel, Pierpoint, John Mills, Meyler, Bradshaw, and others, who seemed to think that the principal object of their existence ought to be that of obtaining notoriety by their dress. In addition to this class, we had a series of fops about town, who were yet more extravagant in their dress and manners.

I well remember Captain T——, in Paris, immediately after the war. He lived in a magnificent style, having taken no less than two different hotels, which naturally created a good deal of gossip in the fashionable world. His carriages and horses were English, and considered the most perfect things of the day. But the most remarkable feature of his eccentricities was the captain's dress: he wore trousers capacious enough for a Turk; his coat, which he always designed himself, was remarkable for its wide, bagged sleeves, and an ingenious mode of making the collar a sort of receptacle for a voluminous quantity of shirt frill; indeed, the shirt collar appeared to descend from his ears all the way down his back, so that you might suppose he was looking out of a black chimney-pot.

Nature had bestowed upon him handsome features, and a profusion of hair, which he had curled and arranged in such an eccentric style that the snaky locks appeared to be always desiring to escape from his head, and were only detained on his cranium by a tight-fitting little hat, suitable for a boy about fourteen. He wore a pair of golden spurs, with rowels of the circumference of a small dessert-plate. Thus he strutted about the streets of Paris, inviting the smiles of those who knew him, and the positive laughter of strangers to whom he was unknown. When Mike Fitzgerald met him for the first time, after the end of the war, he said, "Well, T——, I am happy to find you have won your spurs: made of doubloons, I suppose."

Peace to his ashes! He died in the flower of his age, much regretted by a large circle of friends; and his death was mourned by nearly all the best families of the Faubourg St Germain, with whom he had lived on the most intimate and friendly terms for a quarter of a century.

SHERIDAN AND THE ELECTORS OF STAFFORD.—In my last volume I have spoken of my return as member of Parliament for Stafford. Many circumstances have been brought to my mind lately with regard to Sheridan, who had been one of my predecessors, by my witnessing a wild drama that has been brought on the French stage, under the title of "L'Homme de Rien," which purports to be a biography of that distinguished man. Those who have seen how Mrs Siddons, Edmund Kean, and Dean Swift have been rendered ridiculous by the incredible ignorance of dramatic authors in France about everything English, and of every circumstance of the lives of those they purport to represent, would not be surprised at the liberties they have taken with the great orator, wit, and dramatist.

I heard from some very old men amongst my constituents the singular history of the canvass of Sheridan for this immaculate borough. His reputation had already reached the town, but the defects which unfortunately also rendered him conspicuous were then unknown. He was reported to possess, besides, unbounded influence with the Government, and to have the entire management of Drury Lane Theatre. His voters, being fully convinced that they ought to receive a *quid pro quo* for their "most sweet voices," every one had a favour to ask. One had a son who had great dramatic talent, another was an admirable scene-painter, others had cousins and nephews who would make excellent door-keepers, lamp-lighters, check-takers, or box-openers; there were tailors, *coiffeurs*, and decorators, who could dress with inimitable effect the *dramatis personæ.* Sheridan listened with his usual bland smile to every request, and complied with them all; each individual being furnished with a letter to the stage-manager of Drury Lane, they all started off for the metropolis, full of eager expectation. On their arrival they were favourably received, and each person obtained the situation that he had desired. When letters from London announcing the fulfilment of Sheridan's promises reached the hungry constituents of Stafford, a fresh batch of aspirants for office posted off, and all were equally successful; the consequence was that, on the day of election, the favourite was returned with every demonstration of admiration and confidence.

Scarcely, however, had the member of Parliament left the town than innumerable reproaches were heaped upon his head; it was found that upon application for the payment of the salaries due to the different persons employed there was no money in the treasury. On Saturday night the receipts were carefully handed over to Sheridan, who carelessly spent the money; so that the whole of the humbler *employés* received nothing, whilst the higher order of actors contrived to dun and worry the thoughtless and extravagant *entrepreneur* out of a portion of their salaries.

Great was the indignation excited amongst Sheridan's constituents on finding that they had placed their political interests in the hánds of such a man, and a deputation of three persons was despatched to London to remonstrate with him. They went at a fixed hour to the residence of the great man, where they found a large crowd of his creditors assembled, many of them apparently bent on saying some very disagreeable truths. After waiting for some time, the folding-doors were thrown open, and out stepped the delinquent, in the first style of fashion. Looking around him with a fascinating smile, he addressed a few words to each of his would-be tormentors in succession; each one in his turn was delighted, and quite incapable of making unpleasant observations. They saw before them the man whose speech they had just read in the *Times* and *Courier*, which had proclaimed him in their leading articles the first orator of the age; and they had seen in the *Morning Post* a paragraph describing the irresistible wit which had convulsed Brookes's with laughter, and which concluded by pronouncing the honourable member an ornament to British society.

On this occasion, Sheridan soon observed that the deputation from Stafford was an angry one; so he walked quietly up to each individual, and put some questions to him relating to his domestic concerns. He had not forgotten anybody or any circumstance. He asked one of his constituents if Mrs Grundy's preserves and jams, which she was making when last he saw her, had proved of first-rate quality; whether Miss Grundy the elder continued to charm the world with playing Stiebelt's "Storm" on the piano; if Miss Grundy the younger still took lessons from Mr Town in velvet-painting; and whether Dr Squill had successfully vaccinated Master Tommy. To each the great man had something to say which seemed calculated to soothe the irritation of the hearer, and to prevent him from uttering a word of blame. Each man saw before him the most fascinating individual in the kingdom fixing upon him his dark flashing eye, and addressing him in persuasive accents, with the blandest smile. Sheridan moved through the admiring circle with graceful step, no one venturing to stop him; and as he reached the door he turned round, made an enchanting bow, and having entered his carriage, kissed his hand gracefully to his surrounding friends, and loudly told the coachman to drive to Carlton House. Away he went in a carriage for which the coachmaker had received no money, driven by a coachman and footman whose wages had not been paid for months, but who were still so pleased with their master that they were willing to wait, and in fact rather starve in his service, than live in the family of the richest nobleman upon the fat of the land.

Upon the dissolution of Parliament, Sheridan went down to Stafford; but he found circumstances completely changed; he could not obtain the promise of a single vote from his old friends. In consequence of his continued excesses, he had lost much of the charm of outward appearance that had won him friends at an earlier period; and nothing remained of his once expressive face but the remarkable brilliancy of his eyes; his cheeks were bloated, his nose was of a fiery red, and his general aspect bespoke the self-indulgence of the reckless man. His appearance on the hustings was the signal for a volley of opprobrious terms. One man in the crowd bawled out, "We won't send you to Parliament, for your nose will set the House of Commons on fire;" another had some doggerel rhymes to recite about

> "The Whigs' banners are blue;
> Your nose and your cheeks are red,
> From port-wine and brandy too,
> And there's *sherry* in your head."

In vain did the once-admired orator attempt to gain a hearing; he was driven away amid the derision of the crowd, and never again was enabled to shew his face in Stafford.

It has been said that his first election cost him £2500; but this has been strenuously denied. An anecdote, however, was in circulation, and had reached his biographer, Thomas Moore, to the effect that a deputation from Stafford had waited upon Sheridan, requiring that he should give a vote contrary to his own views, and that his answer was a decided negative, expressed in these words, "Gentlemen, I bought you, and I assure you that I shall sell you whenever it suits my convenience."

Many of the follies and extravagances that marked the life of this gifted but reckless personage must be attributed to the times in which he existed. Drinking was the fashion of the day. The Prince, Mr Pitt, Dundas, the Lord Chancellor Eldon, and many others, who gave the tone to society, would, if they now appeared at an evening party, "as was their custom of an afternoon," be pronounced fit for nothing but bed. A three-bottle man was not an unusual guest at a fashionable table; and the night was invariably spent in drinking bad port-wine to an enormous extent.

SHERIDAN AT DRURY-LANE THEATRE.—However, many of the tricks played by Sheridan were quite unjustifiable. A very old man, and who had suffered severely by his confidence in the great orator, was pointed out to me. On a Friday evening, after the second price had been received, the treasurer of Drury-Lane Theatre came to Sheridan with a wofully long face, and told him that there was not money enough to pay even the subordinates on the following day; and that unless a certain sum could be found he was persuaded that the house could not open on Monday. Sheridan suggested several plans for raising the wind, but all were declared by Mr Dunn to be useless. Sheridan gazed round at the thinly-peopled boxes, and at length called to one of the porters in waiting, "Do you see that stout, good-tempered-looking man seated next a comely lady in the third box from the stage, in a front row? Immediately the play is over, go to him; have a couple of wax candles carried by a boy who can make graceful bows; open the box door, and in a voice loud enough to be heard by every one, say, 'Sir, Mr Sheridan requests *the honour of a private interview* with you in his own room.' Let every one on the way treat him with the greatest civility; and, Mr Dunn, will you have the kindness to see that a bottle of the best port and a couple of wine glasses are placed on the table in my study."

The orders were duly obeyed. The gentleman was ushered into the presence of Sheridan with honours almost approaching those shewn to royalty, and was received by him with the most cordial marks of friendship and regard. "I am always so happy to see any one from Stafford. I was glad you called at my house for an order to this theatre, where I hope you will come when you please; you will find your name on the free list. I think I remember you told me you always came twice a year to London." "Yes," was the reply; "January and July, to receive my dividends." "You have come for that purpose now," continued Sheridan. "Oh, yes; and I went to the Bank of England and got my six hundred pounds." "Ah," said the manager, "you are in Consols, whilst I, alas, am Reduced, and can get nothing till April, when, you know, the interest is paid; and till then I shall be in great distress." "Oh," said his constituent, "let that not make you uneasy; if you give me the power of attorney to receive the money for you when it is due, I can let you have three hundred pounds, which I shall not want till then." "Only a real friend," said Sheridan, shaking his dupe by the hand with warmth, "could have made such a proposition. I accept it thankfully." And the three hundred pounds were immediately transferred from the pocket-book of the unwary man of Stafford into that of the penniless manager of the theatre.

April arrived, a power of attorney was one

morning handed over for signature to Sheridan, whose only reply was, "I never spoke of Consols *in* Reduced, I only spoke of my consols being reduced; unhappy is the man who does not comprehend the weight of prepositions." The Stafford man, burning with indignation, rushed up to London, and found his cajoler calmly seated in his room at Drury Lane. Sheridan, apparently not at all disconcerted, with outstretched hand and benignant smile welcomed his victim, whose rage was at first uncontrollable; but his attack was met by the manager with an acknowledgment that, in a moment of urgent necessity he had been compelled to throw himself on the generosity of a man whom he had heard from every one was a model of worth, and whose acquaintance would be acceptable in the highest quarters. "But excuse me, my dear sir," he added; "I am now commanded to go to the Prince of Wales, to whom I shall narrate your noble conduct. My carriage is waiting, and I can take you to Carlton House." The eye of the provincial sparkled with delight. Was it possible that he meant to take him to the Prince of Wales? It sounded something like it. He shook Sheridan by the hand, saying, "I forgive you, my dear friend; never mention the debt again." "I will take care never to do so," said the manager. The carriage came round to the door, the two friends entered it, and when they arrived at Carlton House, Sheridan got out, and closing the door, told the coachman to drive the gentleman to his hotel. The Stafford man, with a last hope, naïvely said, "I thought I also was going into Carlton House." "Another mistake of yours," replied Sheridan. The worthy constituent returned that night to Stafford; and in future his vote was given against Sheridan.

Shelley's Fight at Eton.—In the year 1809 an incident occurred at Eton which caused no small sensation and merriment throughout the school. It was announced one morning that Shelley, the future poet, had actually accepted wager of battle from Sir Thomas Styles. Whether he had received an insult, and that vast disparity in size gave him confidence, or that, over-full of the warlike descriptions of Homer's heroes, he was fired to imitate their exploits against some one or other, remains a secret. Meet, however, they did, after twelve, in the playing-fields. The usual preliminaries were arranged—a ring was formed, seconds and bottle-holders were all in readiness, and the combatants stood face to face. The tall, lank figure of the poet towered above the diminutive, thick-set little Baronet, by nearly a head and shoulders. In the first round no mischief was done; Sir Thomas seemed to be feeling his way, being naturally desirous of ascertaining what his gigantic adversary was made of; and Shelley, though brandishing his long arms, had evidently no idea of their use in a pugilistic point of view. After a certain amount of sparring without effect, the combatants were invited by their seconds to take breath. The Baronet did not hesitate to accept the offer to sit upon the knee of his second; but Shelley disdainfully declined to rest, and, calculating upon finishing the fight by a single blow, stalked round the ring, looking defiance at his little adversary.

Time was called, and the battle was renewed in earnest. The Baronet, somewhat cautious, planted his first blow upon the chest of Shelley, who did not appear to relish it. However, though not a proficient in the art of self-defence, he nevertheless went in, and knocked the little Baronet off his legs, who lay sprawling upon the grass more dead than alive. Shelley's confidence increased; he stalked round the ring as before, and spouted one of the defiant addresses usual with Homer's heroes when about to commence a single combat: the young poet, being a first-rate classical scholar, actually delivered the speech in the original Greek, to the no small amusement of the boys. In the second and last round, Styles went to work like a first-rate artist, and, after several slighter blows, delivered what is called in the prize-ring "a heavy slogger" on Shelley's bread-basket; this seemed positively to electrify the bard, for, I blush to say, he broke through the ring, and took to his heels with a speed that defied pursuit. His seconds, backers, and all who had witnessed the fight, joined in full cry after him, but he outran them all, and got safe to the house of his tutor, Mr Bethel.

This incident naturally excited much merriment at Eton at the time, and Shelley never more, during his stay at college, ventured to enter the pugilistic arena, but passed his leisure hours in making various experiments in chemistry and natural science. He even went so far as to employ a travelling tinker to assist him in making a miniature steam-engine, which burst, and very nearly blew the bard and the Bethel family into the air.

EPIGRAM BY CANNING. — When Tomlyn, the Bishop of Winchester, died, every effort was made by Pelham to succeed to the bishopric. The following epigram was written by Canning :—

"Says priggish Pelham, 'May I beg a hint on
The shortest road from Exeter to Winton ?' *
Says Bloomfield,† 'Sure you cannot fail to light on
The shortest road through *Hertford*‡ and through Brighton.'"

Mr Canning and Lord Lyndhurst.—When George Canning succeeded Lord Liverpool as Premier, he was at a loss to find a Chancellor. He had quarrelled with Copley (Lord Lyndhurst) a few nights before, for having, in a violent speech, inveighed against the Catholics in no measured terms: Canning had even accused him of having learnt by heart a pamphlet, published the day before, by the Bishop of Exeter against the Catholics. Nevertheless, Canning, when forming his ministry, wrote the following laconic note to Copley:—"*Non obstante Philpotto,* will you be my Chancellor?" The bait took, and Copley the same day became Chancellor, and forty-eight hours after was gazetted Lord Lyndhurst.

Crockford's Club.—I have alluded, in my first volume, to the high play which took place at White's and Brookes's in the olden time, and at Wattier's in the days of Brummel and the dandies. Charles

* Winton, the old name of Winchester.

† Sir B. Bloomfield, afterwards Lord Bloomfield, a great favourite of the Prince Regent's.

‡ The *Marchioness.*

Fox, George Selwyn, Lord Carlisle, Fitzpatrick, Horace Walpole, the Duke of Queensberry, and others, lost whole fortunes at faro, macao, and hazard; almost the only winners, indeed, of that generation were General Scott, father-in-law of Canning, the Duke of Portland, and Lord Robert Spencer: Lord Robert, indeed, bought the beautiful estate of Woolbidding, in Sussex, with the proceeds of his gains by keeping the bank at Brookes's.

But, in the reign of George IV., a new star rose upon the horizon in the person of Mr William Crockford; and the old-fashioned games of faro, macao, and lansquenet gave place to the all-devouring thirst for the game of hazard. Crockey, when still a young man, had relinquished the peaceful trade of a fishmonger for a share in a "hell," where, with his partner Gye, he managed to win, after a sitting of twenty-four hours, the enormous sum of one hundred thousand pounds from Lords Thanet and Granville, Mr Ball Hughes, and two other gentlemen whose names I do not now remember. With this capital added to his former gains, he built the well-known palace in St James's Street, where a club was established and play organised on a scale of magnificence and liberality hitherto unknown in Europe.

One may safely say, without exaggeration, that

Crockford won the whole of the ready money of the then existing generation. As is often the case at Lords' Cricket-ground, the great match of the gentlemen of England against the professional players was won by the latter. It was a very hollow thing, and in a few years twelve hundred thousand pounds were swept away by the fortunate fishmonger. He did not, however, die worth more than a sixth part of this vast sum; the difference being swallowed up in various unlucky speculations.

No one can describe the splendour and excitement of the early days of Crockey. A supper of the most exquisite kind, prepared by the famous Ude, and accompanied by the best wines in the world, together with every luxury of the season, was furnished gratis. The members of the club included all the celebrities of England, from the Duke of Wellington to the youngest Ensign of the Guards; and at the gay and festive board, which was constantly replenished from midnight to early dawn, the most brilliant sallies of wit, the most agreeable conversation, the most interesting anecdotes, interspersed with grave political discussions and acute logical reasoning on every conceivable subject, proceeded from the soldiers, scholars, statesmen, poets, and men of pleasure, who, when the "house was up" and balls and parties at an end, delighted to finish their evening with a little supper and a good deal of hazard at old Crockey's. The tone of the club was excellent. A most gentlemanlike feeling prevailed, and none of the rudeness, familiarity, and ill-breeding which disgrace some of the minor clubs of the present day, would have been tolerated for a moment.

Though not many years have elapsed since the time of which I write, the supper-table had a very different appearance from what it would present did the club now exist. Beards were completely unknown, and the rare mustachios were only worn by officers of the Household Brigade or hussar regiments. Stiff white neckcloths, blue coats and brass buttons, rather short-waisted white waistcoats, and tremendously embroidered shirt-fronts with gorgeous studs of great value, were considered the right thing. A late deservedly popular Colonel in the Guards used to give Storr and Mortimer £25 a year to furnish him with a new set of studs every Saturday night during the London season.

The great foreign diplomatists, Prince Talleyrand, Count Pozzo di Borgo, General Alava, the Duke of Palmella, Prince Esterhazy, the French, Russian, Spanish, Portuguese, and Austrian ambassadors, and all persons of distinction and eminence who arrived in England, belonged to Crockford's as a matter of course; but many rued the day when they became members of that fascinating but dangerous coterie. The great Duke himself, always rather a friend of the dandies, did not disdain to appear now and then at this charming club; whilst the late Lord Raglan, Lord Anglesey, Sir Hussey Vivian, and many more of our Peninsula and Waterloo heroes, were constant visitors. The two great novelists of the day, who have since become great statesmen, Disraeli and Bulwer Lytton, displayed at that brilliant supper-table the one his sable, the other his auburn curls; there Horace Twiss made proof of an appetite, and Edward Montague of a thirst, which astonished all beholders; whilst the bitter jests of Sir Joseph Copley, Colonel Armstrong, and John Wilson Croker, and the brilliant wit of Alvanley, were the delight of all present, and their *bons mots* were the next day retailed all over England.

In the play-room might be heard the clear ringing voice of that agreeable reprobate, Tom Duncombe, as he cheerfully called, "Seven," and the powerful hand of the vigorous Sefton in throwing for a ten. There might be noted the scientific dribbling of a four by "King" Allen, the tremendous backing of nines and fives by Ball Hughes and Auriol, the enormous stakes played for by Lords Lichfield and Chesterfield, George

Payne, Sir St Vincent Cotton, D'Orsay, and George Anson, and, above all, the gentlemanly bearing and calm and unmoved demeanour, under losses or gains, of all the men of that generation.

The old fishmonger himself, seated snug and sly at his desk in the corner of the room, watchful as the dragon that guarded the golden apples of the Hesperides, would only give credit to sure and approved signatures. Who that ever entered that dangerous little room can ever forget the large green table with the croupiers, Page, Darking, and Bacon, with their suave manners, sleek appearance, stiff white neckcloths, and the almost miraculous quickness and dexterity with which they swept away the money of the unfortunate punters when the fatal cry of "Deuce ace," "Aces," or "Sixes out," was heard in answer to the caster's bold cry of "Seven," or "Nine," or "Five 's the main."

O noctes cœnæque deûm! but the brightest medal has its reverse, and after all the wit and gaiety and excitement of the night, how disagreeable the waking up, and how very unpleasant the sight of the little card, with its numerous figures marked down on the debtor side in the fine bold hand of Mr Page. Alas, poor Crockey's! shorn of its former glory, has become a sort of refuge for the destitute, a cheap dining-house. How are the mighty fallen! Irish buckeens, spring captains, "welchers" from Newmarket, and suspicious-looking foreigners, may be seen swaggering, after dinner, through the marble halls and up that gorgeous staircase where once the chivalry of England loved to congregate; and those who remember Crockford's in all its glory, cast, as they pass, a look of unavailing regret at its dingy walls, with many a sigh to the memory of the pleasant days they passed there, and the gay companions and noble gentlemen who have long since gone to their last home.

"KING" ALLEN.—The late Viscount Allen, commonly called "King" Allen, was a well-known character in London for many years. He was a tall, stout, and pompous-looking personage, remarkably well got up, with an invariably new-looking hat and well-polished boots. His only exercise and usual walk was from White's to Crockford's, and from Crockford's to White's.

Who in this ponderous old man would have recognised the gallant youth who, as Ensign in the Guards, led on his men with incredible energy and activity across the ravine at Talavera; where, if the great Duke had not sent the 48th Regiment to their assistance, very little more would have been heard of "King" Allen and his merry men? But one of the most famous dandies of his day was not fated thus to perish; and he was preserved for thirty years after the great battle, to swagger down Bond Street or lounge on the sunny side of Pall Mall, to become an *arbiter elegantiarum* amongst the tailors, and a Mæcenas at the opera and play.

To render the "King" perfectly happy, one little item was wanting—money. His estates, if he ever had any, had long passed from him, and he had much difficulty in making the two ends meet. When, for economy's sake, he was obliged to retire for a short time to Dublin, he had a very large door in Merrion Square, with an almost equally large brass plate, on which his name was engraved in letters of vast size; but it was very much doubted whether there was any house behind it. He was a great diner out; and one spiteful old lady, whom he had irritated by some uncivil remarks, told him that his title was as good as board wages to him.

Strange to say, this *mauvais sujet* was a great friend of the late Sir Robert Peel, when Chief Secretary for Ireland; and on one occasion, when they were proceeding in an open carriage to dine with a friend a few miles from Dublin, in passing through a village, they had the misfortune to drive over the oldest inhabitant, an ancient beldam, who was generally stationed on the bridge. A large mob gathered round the carriage; and as Peel and the Tory Government were very unpopular at the period to which I refer, the mob began to grow abusive, and cast very threatening and ominous looks at the occupants of the barouche; when the "King," with a coolness and self-possession worthy of Brummel, rose up, displaying an acre of white waistcoat, and called out, "Now, postboy, go on, and don't drive over any more old women." The mob, awe-struck by "King" Allen's majestic deportment, retired, and "the industrious and idle apprentices" went on their way rejoicing.

The "King" was not a very good-natured person; and as he had a strong inclination to, and some talent for, sarcasm, he made himself many enemies. To give an idea of his "style." When the statue of George III. was erected in front of Ransom's banking-house, Mr Williams, one of the partners, commonly known by the name of "Swell Bill," petitioned the Woods and Forests to remove that work of art, as it collected a crowd of little boys, who were peculiarly facetious on the subject of the pigtail of that obstinate but domestic monarch, and otherwise obstructed business. Lord Allen, meeting Williams at White's, said, "I should have thought the erection of the statue rather an advantage to you, because, while you are standing idle at your own shop door, it would prevent you seeing the crowds hurrying to the respectable establishment of Messrs Coutts & Co., close by in the Strand."

The "King" did not possess much wit, but no one could say more disagreeable things at the most disagreeable moment. I remember his setting down the late Lady N——, daughter-in-law of a celebrated legal functionary of that name, in rather an amusing manner. She was a vulgar Irish grazier's daughter, extremely plain, and clipped the King's English in a vain attempt to conceal a mellifluous King's County brogue. After passing many years in Rutland Square, Dublin, she suddenly found herself a Countess, with a large income. Her first step after this accession of dignity and fortune was to start for London, where she affected to have passed her life. On meeting Lord Allen soon after her arrival, she extended one finger of her little fat hand, and in a drawling, affected tone of voice said, "My Lard Alleen, how long have you been in London?" "Forty years, ma'am," growled out the "King."

Lord Allen greatly resembled in later life an ancient grey parrot, both in the aquiline outline of his features, and his peculiar mode of walking, with one foot crossed over the other in a slow and wary manner. He was a regular Cockney, and very seldom left London; but on one occasion, when he had gone down with Alvanley to Dover for the sake of his health, and complained to his facetious friend that he could get no sleep, Alvanley ordered a coach to drive up and down in front of the inn windows all night, and made the boots call out, in imitation of the London watchmen of that day, "Half-past two, and a stormy night." The well-known rumble of the wheels, and the dulcet tones of the boots, had the desired effect; the "King" passed excellent nights, and was soon able to return to his little house in South Street with renewed health and spirits.

Lord Allen was at last obliged to leave London, after coming to an understanding with his creditors; and after passing some time at Cadiz, died at Gibraltar in 1843, when his title became extinct.

Ball Hughes.—I was at Eton with my late friend Ball Hughes, whose recent death was so much lamented in Paris. He was known at Eton by the name of Ball only; but the year before he came of age, he took the additional name of Hughes, his uncle, Admiral Hughes, having left him the fortune he had amassed during his command of the fleet on the Indian seas, and which was supposed to be not less than forty thousand a year. But Hughes entered the army early in life, his uncle having bought him a commission in the 7th Hussars, and made him a handsome allowance. He was a great imitator of the Colonel of his regiment, the Earl of Uxbridge, afterwards Marquis of Anglesea, whom he took as a model for his coats, hats, and boots; indeed everything that his noble commander said or did was law to him. Hughes was a remarkably handsome man, and made a considerable figure in the best society; his manners were excellent; he was a thoroughly amiable, agreeable fellow, and universally popular.

When he came into his fortune, he was considered a great match by all the women in London. He fell desperately in love with Lady Jane Paget, the daughter of his Colonel, and the marriage-settlements were all arranged; but, unluckily for the disappointed lover, Lady Jane, at the last moment, gave a most decided negative, and the match was broken off. Ball was not long disconsolate, but looking around him, fixed his attention upon the lovely Miss Floyd, who afterwards married Sir Robert Peel; finding his attentions unacceptable in that quarter, he proposed to Lady Caroline Churchill, afterwards Lady Caroline Pennant, but here he was refused. This, however, did not prevent him from being considered an eligible match by a great many mothers, who diligently sought his society. He was courted, followed, and admired by every one who had daughters to dispose of; but, unfortunately for him, the young ladies, having heard of his numerous disappointments, were not ready to unite their fate with a man whose rejected addresses were so well known. "The Golden Ball," as he was called, continued, nevertheless, to make his appearance everywhere. He was devoted to female society; no dinner, ball, pic-nic, or party, was complete unless the popular millionaire formed one of the social circle.

Ball Hughes's first step, on entering into possession of his fortune, was to employ Mr Wyatt the architect to furnish a mansion for him in Brook Street. No expense was spared to make it as near perfection as possible. Wyatt had a *carte-blanche,* and bought for him buhl furniture, rich hangings, statues, bronzes, and works of art to an extent that made an inroad even upon his wealth.

A beautiful Spanish *danseuse,* named Mercandotti, arrived about this time in London, in the midst of the gay season of 1822, under the immediate patronage of Lord Fife. She was then only fifteen years of age, and by some she was believed to be his daughter, by others only his *protégée.* At Barcelona she was considered inimitable; at Madrid she gained great applause; in Seville she acquired immense reputation; and by the time the lovely girl reached London, great curiosity was excited to see the new candidate for public favour at the King's Theatre, where she was engaged for the season at £800. The new *débutante* met with complete success, and was pronounced divine. All the dandies who had the *entrée* behind the scenes surrounded her and paid her homage, and more than one scion of the fashionable world offered to surrender his liberty for life to the fascinating dancer. Ebers, then manager of the theatre, was pestered from morning to night by young men of fashion anxious to obtain an introduction to Mademoiselle Mercandotti, but they were invariably referred by the *impresario* to Lord Fife.

One night, March 8, 1823, the house was enormously crowded by an audience eager to see the favourite in the then popular ballet by Auber, "Alfred;" when just before the curtain drew up, the manager came forward and expressed his regret that Mademoiselle Mercandotti had disappeared, and that he had been unable to discover where she had gone. Knowing ones, however, guessed that she had been carried off by the "Golden Ball," whose advances had been very favourably received, and who had evidently made a strong impression upon the damsel;

and a few days after, the *Morning Post* announced that a marriage had taken place between a young man of large fortune and one of the most remarkable dancers of the age. The persons present at the marriage were the mother of the bride, Mr Ebers, and Lord Fife. The honeymoon was passed at Oatlands, which the happy bridegroom had shortly before purchased from the Duke of York.

Ainsworth wrote the following epigram on this event :—

> "The fair damsel is gone ; and no wonder at all
> That, bred to the dance, she is gone to a Ball."

Ball Hughes died at St Germains two years ago. His fortune had dwindled down to a fourth of its original amount, for he was perhaps the greatest gambler of his day. His love of play was such, that at one period of his life he would rather play at pitch and toss than be without his favourite excitement. He told me that at one time he had lost considerable sums at battledoor and shuttlecock. On one occasion, immediately after dinner, he and the eccentric Lord Petersham commenced playing with these toys, and continued hard at work during the whole of the night; next morning he was found by his valet lying on the ground, fast asleep, but ready for any other species of speculation. His purchase of Oatlands, which at the time was considered a foolish one, proved a very good speculation; for it was sold, for building villas, for so large a sum, that Hughes, whose fortune had dwindled to a mere pittance, became in his latter days very well off again; and though he lived in retirement, kept a large establishment, and was in the enjoyment of every luxury.

SCROPE DAVIES.—The name of Scrope Davies is now but little known, except in connexion with Brummell's exit from the fashionable world of London, and from his being occasionally mentioned by Lord Byron and by Moore; yet few men were better received in society, or more the fashion than he once was. He was educated at Eton, and from thence he migrated in due time to King's College, Cambridge, of which he became a fellow; there he formed those acquaintance that at a later period served as an introduction into that world of which he soon became a distinguished ornament. His manners and appearance were of the true Brummell type: there was nothing showy in his exterior. He was quiet and reserved in ordinary company, but he was the life and soul of those who relished learning and wit; being a ripe scholar, and well read, he was always ready with an apt quotation.

As was the case with many of the foremost men

of that day, the greater number of his hours were passed at the gambling-table, where for a length of time he was eminently successful; for he was a first-rate calculator. He seldom played against individuals; he preferred going to the regular establishments. But on one occasion he had, by a remarkable run of good luck, completely ruined a young man who had just reached his majority and come into the possession of a considerable fortune. The poor youth sank down upon a sofa in abject misery, when he reflected that he was a beggar; for he was on the point of marriage. Scrope Davies, touched by his despair, entered into conversation with him, and ended by giving him back the whole of his losses, upon a solemn promise that he never would play again. The only thing that Scrope retained of his winnings was one of the little carriages of that day, called a dormeuse, from its being fitted up with a bed, for he said, "When I travel in it I shall sleep the better for having acted rightly." The youth kept his promise; but when his benefactor wanted money, he forgot that he owed all he possessed to Scrope's generosity, and refused to assist him.

For a long time Scrope Davies was a lucky player; but the time arrived when Fortune deserted her old favourite; and, shortly after the Dandy dynasty was overthrown, he found himself unable to mingle with the rich, the giddy, and the gay. With the wreck of his fortune, and indeed but little to live upon beyond the amount of his own Cambridge fellowship, he sought repose in Paris, and there, indulging in literary leisure, bade the world farewell. He had but few intimates, and those only whom he had formerly known in his days of affluence.

He was a great admirer of Moore, and when some one said the poet had incurred reproach for writing "Little's" Poems, Scrope said the Roman poet has best expressed himself on that subject: *Ubi plura nitent, non ego paucis offendar maculis;* which he thus translated, "Moore shines so brightly that I cannot find fault with Little's vagaries." He also said, *Ne plus ultra*—nothing is better than Moore. Somebody observing that Moore was a true Irish name, but it was nothing without the addition of O, "Oh," replied Scrope, "I always thought that O'thello, Moor of Venice, was an Irishman, from the blunders that he made." He remarked, on one occasion, "You can find in Shakespeare an apt expression for everything that this earth affords." Somebody asked, "Where does Shakespeare ever allude to the tread-mill?" "Oh," answered Scrope, "you will find in 'King Lear' the words, 'Down, down, thou climbing sorrow!'" "Not an exact quotation," retorted one who was present.

"Yes," said Scrope; "but the old king was in a rage when he expressed himself."

Scrope Davies bore with perfect resignation the loss of the wealth he had once possessed; and though his annual income was very limited, he made no complaint of poverty. He daily sat himself down on a bench in the garden of the Tuileries, where he received those whose acquaintance he desired, and then returned to his study, where he wrote notes upon the men of his day, which have unfortunately disappeared: that they existed there can be no doubt, as he occasionally read extracts from his diary to those in whom he placed confidence. Ball Hughes was about the last of his visitors. Scrope found the former gay young man very much improved in mind by adversity, and was wont to say, "He is no longer 'Golden Ball;' but since the gilt is off, he rolls on much more smoothly than he did." Having heard that Brummell had obtained a consulship when Lord Melbourne came into office, Scrope went over to London and had an interview with the noble Lord; but he told his friends, "Lamb looked so sheepish when I was ushered into his presence, that I asked him for nothing; indeed there were so many nibbling at his grass, that I felt I ought not to jump over the fence into the meadow upon which such animals were feeding."

Thomas Moore.—During my residence in Paris, several distinguished men took up their abode for a time, and were universally well received. Thomas Moore stayed for a considerable length of time, and his diary, admirably edited by Lord John Russell, shews most minutely how his hours were spent, and the people with whom he mingled. He was a favourite guest everywhere, but he was attracted only where a good *cuisine* would satisfy the taste of the *gourmet.* He realised (at least in Paris) Sir Edward Lytton Bulwer's admirable conception of Lord Guloseton, in his ever favourite novel, "Pelham." When Moore had received an invitation to dinner from an untried Amphitryon, previous to returning an answer he cross-examined all who visited him. Had his friend an established kitchen, with a *chef* of his own? or did he depend upon a neighbouring *restaurateur?* Did the *chef* deserve the name of an *artiste?* Were the wines of a choice quality? Did they come direct from wine-growing countries? or were they likely to be the product of some Parisian wine-doctor? All these questions were asked with a serious earnestness that exhibited the great poet's exquisite taste in the pleasures of the table. It must, however, be added, that he was equally anxious that the invited should be intellectual or distinguished persons; and one stipulation in accepting the invitation was that English should be the language of the table: nothing seemed to annoy him more thoroughly than to find that, for the sake of a single individual, French should be the order of the day.

Whatever might be his peculiarities and his demands, however, they were amply repaid by the brilliancy of his conversation and the charm of his manners. He would now and then, when entirely at his ease with well-known friends, give an imitation of the great Irish orator Curran, which those who had known the original pronounced to be perfect, while those who had never seen him were delighted with the wit and humour that were introduced; but it was when the dinner was ended, the drawing-room reached, and a few of his much loved country-women were present, that the charm of Moore's society was felt. Almost without an invitation he would unaffectedly sit down to the pianoforte and warble forth some of those enchanting melodies which he has given to a grateful nation, accompanying himself with exquisite taste; his voice was rich in tone, and the expression he threw into his own words, combined with his beaming face and genial manner, elicited the admiration of all. Those who have heard him sing "Those Evening Bells," and "Oft in the Stilly Night," will carry a recollection of one of the most agreeable moments of their lives. He fully deserved the cognomen of "Anacreon," by which he was much known in Parisian society. The French are accustomed to Christian names of Greek origin; they have Achilles, Hector, and I have known several Nestors and one Epaminondas: indeed it is their not unfrequent custom to drop the surname. Many men are distinguished entirely by the prenomen; and as "Anacreon" Moore had been the sobriquet of the illustrious Irish lyric poet, from the time of his translation of the classic bard, he was soon christened "Anacreon," and as such generally known.

I remember once visiting M. Sommarivas's collection, and on mounting the staircase, the domestic whispered into my ear that "Monsieur Anacreon" was in one of the saloons; as that name had not then reached my ears, I asked him who was "Monsieur Anacreon;" the man looked at me with something like astonishment at the question, and after a short pause said, "It is your great English Béranger that is looking at our collection." On entering the saloon my mind was enlightened by recognising the bard of Erin, who, with animated looks and lively gestures, was pointing out the beauties of an antique statue; he wore the earnest and intellectual expression which distinguished him when delighting his friends with a barcarolle, or one of his sweetest melodies. Moore always heard with infinite pleasure any compliment paid to his wife; indeed one of his most remarkable characteristics was his intense fondness for her; he was in fact the most uxorious of mortals, and though he could smile on any pretty woman, all his affections were centred in his charming "Bessy."

FRANCIS HARE. — Francis Hare, sarcastically nicknamed "The Silent Hare," from his extreme loquacity, was remarkable for his leanness, his appetite, and his conversational powers. He could not only speak every European language, but all the various *patois* of each tongue, with a rapid and effervescent utterance that reminded one of the rushing of some alpine torrent, or Pyreneean *Gave* battling with the impediments that obstruct its course. His memory was as surprising as his loquacity; he could repeat whole pages from almost any book that was mentioned in his presence, and "come down" with effect on any unlucky wight who had made an incorrect quotation from some rare or obsolete volume, which might have been supposed to be unknown to all present.

One day, in a country house, his friends had made a bet that they would catch him napping, and start a subject on which he could have nothing to say. With this view they read up an article in an encyclopædia of that time, on Chinese music. At dinner one of the conspirators introduced the subject, a second took it up, and a third exhausted the knowledge they had gained by reading the learned essay. To their intense astonishment, Hare, in his excited, spluttering manner, took up the topic, contradicted all the statements that had been made, proved that they were all in the wrong, and concluded by saying, "I see, my good fellows, where you have taken your impressions about the harmony of the Celestial Empire. You have found them in an article in such an encyclopædia, which I myself wrote ten years ago; but since then I have studied the subject and conversed with well-informed travellers, and I have arrived at conclusions diametrically opposed to those I held when I wrote the article."*

Hare was very fond of practical jokes and mystifications of all sorts. While passing a winter at Pisa, he amused himself, (rather sacrilegiously, I must admit,) one day that he was visiting the baptistry, by entering a confessional. In this quiet old town the priests have a good deal of rustic simplicity about them, and doubtless Hare would never have attempted the same joke either at Florence or Rome, where tales of deadly crimes are too common to astonish the confessor.

Hare, having selected a round-faced, innocent-

* This anecdote is also told of Professor Whewell, the Master of Trinity.

looking priest as his victim, went up to the confessional, knelt down with a look of penitential sorrow, and poured forth in the purest Tuscan the most hideous tale of guilt that ever reached a good father's ear: robbery, blasphemy, sacrilege, rape, and murder were owned to in quick and horrifying succession; till at last the fat priest's placid countenance wore an expression of frantic terror, and opening the other door of the confessional, without cap or breviary, he rushed from the place, and tore down the street, never stopping till he had reached his own dwelling.

In mentioning the name of Hare, I am reminded of a circumstance which occurred to him during the Hundred Days. The English, including our embassy, were so frightened at the unexpected return of the Emperor, that they fled from France as if Old Nick had made his appearance. Hare, on the contrary, remained, and at the first levee held by Napoleon, he made his appearance at the Tuileries, where he was presented to his Majesty.

Napoleon addressed him in the following words:—"Well, sir, what has kept you in Paris, when your countrymen have all left?" "To see the greatest man in Europe, sir." "Ah, it is, then, your opinion, having seen and conversed with me, that I am not that wild beast I am represented to be by your ministers and the members of your Houses of Parliament." "Oh no, sir, it cannot be the opinion of the English ministers; but I blush when I call to mind the manner in which your name has been traduced by our garrulous members of both Houses."

This little episode, and the remarks said to have been made by Hare, reached London in an incredibly short time, when our newspapers attacked him in no measured terms, stating that he was a traitor to his country, and ought to be prosecuted forthwith. But Hare could afford to laugh at their abuse and threats; and on his return to England after the fall of Napoleon, used often to relate with pleasure, and not without some emotion, the conversation he had held with the great French Emperor.

THEODORE HOOK.—I remember being present at a dinner in London, when a very severe and saturnine Scotch Presbyterian was abusing Sunday newspapers, and concluded a violent tirade by saying, "I am determined to set my face against them." "So am I," said Theodore Hook, "every Sunday morning." He was well known at that time to be the editor of the *John Bull* weekly journal.

COSWAY THE PAINTER.—The miniature painter

Cosway enjoyed the reputation of drawing the long bow to a remarkable extent. He was once relating, in my presence, to a large party of incredulous listeners, the story of a boy who had fallen from the top of a church steeple without sustaining any material injury. When he had come to a conclusion, there were a few murmurs, expressive of doubt as to the possibility of such a miraculous preservation, when Cosway, looking round on the company with a glance of solemn defiance, exclaimed, "I was that boy!"

MARTIN HAWKE.—The Hon. Martin Hawke was a remarkable character, of a somewhat original and eccentric turn of mind. He lived many years abroad, and was the principal person who introduced, and rendered popular on the Continent, horse-racing, cricket, and other manly sports. He was well known in Paris, Tours, and Boulogne. He was an excellent horseman, a first-rate pugilist, a capital shot, was passionately fond of field sports, and had a great aversion to anything in the shape of poaching. He had several very serious encounters in France with some very rough customers, whom he found shooting on the manors he had hired; and nothing but his great strength and courage prevented him from falling a sacrifice to their vengeance. Upon one occasion he discovered, to his great joy, a net, which had been set near a wood the night before, and was full of woodcocks. He placed them in his greatcoat pocket, and, arriving at the market-place at Boulogne, where several of his friends had congregated, he addressed them thus :—"Gentlemen, I will shew you a strange sight—some live woodcocks." His friends laughed, and rallied him for endeavouring to impose upon their credulity. In an instant out flew, from his greatcoat pocket, several woodcocks. Brooke Richmond, who squinted a little, asked Martin for one of the cocks, upon which Martin replied, "My good fellow, they have all flown away—except the one in your eye."

When in Paris some forty years back, Hawke received, through Sir C. Stewart, our ambassador, an invitation to accompany the Duc de Berri on a shooting excursion in the forest of St Germain. Prior to the chase, Alexandre de Girardin, the grand *veneur*, or huntsman, informed the gentlemen who were invited that it was not etiquette for them to fire before his Royal Highness had discharged his gun. As bad luck would have it, Hawke, in the ardour of the moment, had completely forgotten the hint given him ; for on the first cock-pheasant getting up, Hawke, who was rather quicker than the royal sportsman, knocked it over close to the feet of the Duke, who in a great rage cried out, in English, "Who the devil are you, sir, who have disobeyed my orders?" Martin, rather ashamed, mentioned his name. The Duke replied, "A droll name yours is, Mr 'Hock;'" upon which Martin, nothing abashed, said, "Oh, sir, your Royal Highness must be acquainted with it already, for my grandfather Admiral Hawke's name was well known in the French navy." The Duc de Berri took this retort very good-humouredly, and said, "Well, well, Mr Hawke, you are a plain-spoken sort of fellow: I like your frankness and spirit, and therefore hope, the next time I have a shooting party at St Germain, you will accompany me again." Alas! the following night the good-natured Prince, on entering the opera, was assassinated by Louvel.

LORD NORMANBY.—The first time I ever saw Lord Normanby was in 1816, during a morning visit at the Right Hon. George Tierney's, in Stratton Street. He was then a remarkably pleasing and good-looking young man; and I remember a circumstance which may account for his entering political life as a Liberal.

His father, Lord Mulgrave, was a high Tory, had long been a member of the administration of Pitt and his successors, and at the time of which

I speak he was Master-General of the Ordnance. On the occasion to which I refer, Lord Normanby, in the course of conversation, informed those present that his father had in a most unceremonious manner been dismissed from his high post to make way for the Duke of Wellington. He denounced, in the bitterest terms, the conduct of the Government towards so old a public servant as his father, and swore he never would forgive them.

He shortly afterwards entered Parliament as an advanced Liberal, always voted with the Whigs; and when they came into office in 1830, he was appointed Governor of Jamaica. On his return thence to England, he filled the post of Lord-Lieutenant of Ireland, under very difficult circumstances, and at a period of great importance, with general applause. His pleasing and conciliating manners made him a general favourite; and the Vice-Regal Court during his stay was a very brilliant one. He afterwards became Secretary of State; and in 1847, ambassador at Paris. He conducted himself with considerable tact, and shewed a certain amount of ability during the latter part of the reign of Louis Philippe. On the establishment of the Republic, he had the good sense to keep quiet, and to remain on good terms with the poets, wood-merchants, and journalists who successively held office. But I do not think he conducted his relations with the present Emperor in a very adroit manner. He misjudged the Prince's capacity and character, and assumed rather a protecting tone with him; and when the *coup d'état* took place, he did not believe that Lord Palmerston would, with his usual decision and foresight, recognise Louis Napoleon as Emperor, immediately the choice of the French nation became known. Lord Normanby afterwards engaged in intrigues against his chief at the Foreign Office, and the latter period of his embassy was not a very satisfactory one, either to himself or to his admirers.

On his resignation, and after an attack of paralysis, he was appointed minister to Florence. This post was given him in lieu of a retiring pension, and because the climate suited him; and Lord Normanby, with his palazzo in town and the Villa Normanby near Fiesole, recalled to his old friends the pleasant days they had spent with him thirty years before, when he resided there as a private gentleman before his accession to office, and when his theatricals were the delight of all who visited Italy.

On the accession of the Tories to power, Lord Normanby and Lord Howden, our envoy to Madrid, were, with an unparalleled want of courtesy, immediately informed by a telegraphic despatch that Her Majesty had no longer any occasion for their services. The insulting nature of this dismissal at the hands of Lord Malmesbury had no effect upon the fixed determination of Lord Normanby to leave his old friends the Whigs. It is supposed that the immense success of the paternal governments of Naples, Florence, Parma, Lucca, and Modena, in making their people happy and contented, must have produced this change in Lord Normanby's opinions; for, immediately on his return to England, he became a most violent Tory; and in his frequent speeches in the House of Lords arraigned and attacked on all occasions the foreign policy of the Whigs, and that with a blind and almost rabid violence, and a degree of bitterness and ill nature, which astonished and disgusted his old friends.

Let us hope that this extraordinary change both in the opinions and feelings of so generally popular and amiable a man was the effect of disease, and attributable to the severe attack of illness from which he had suffered for several years before his death. He was *the* man of all others who should *not* have left the Liberal party. He was the spoiled child of the Whigs, and had received from them every great appointment and every distinction it was in their power to give. Besides the high offices I have before enumerated, he was made a Marquis, a Grand Cross of the Bath, and a Knight of the Garter.

I remember, apropos of this, that when Lord Melbourne was minister, Edward Ellice and the Premier were looking one morning from the windows of the first Lord's residence in Downing Street into St James's Park, and saw Lord Normanby approaching. On Mr Ellice inquiring what he could be coming for, Lord Melbourne said, in his off-hand manner, "I don't know what the devil the fellow can want, unless he comes to ask for a second garter for his other leg." In fact, the commonest gratitude should have made Lord Normanby pause before he took the fatal step which sullied the close of his political career.

Let me turn from this last lamentable error, and remember only his many good and amiable qualities. He was certainly one of the most courteous and agreeable of our ministers and diplomatists. There was no hauteur or reserve in his manner, and yet a natural dignity which prevented all undue familiarity. He was a fluent and ready speaker, and wrote with ease and elegance. When in Dublin he was much beloved by all around him, for he was a thoroughly good-natured man; and because this expression has been often misunderstood and supposed to mean weak or silly, let us not despise this rare and precious gift, much oftener bestowed on men of intellect than on fools. Till his illness, Lord Normanby was never heard to say an unkind thing of any one; and though in the latter years of his life he carried this amiable quality too far, when he took the part of the ex-King of Naples, the Duke of Modena, the Pope, and the brigands and assassins of Antonelli and Merode, yet this kindness in the days of his prosperity had a winning charm, because it was genuine, and sprang from a really good heart.

Had Lord Normanby not taken to politics and become a Viceroy and Secretary of State, he would have achieved great success as a literary man. His two novels, "Matilda," and "Yes and No," were worthy to be placed on a par with the best of their day; and had he been obliged to earn his bread, he might have been a Bulwer or a Kemble. For besides his literary acquirements, he had a remarkable talent for acting; and his theatre at Florence, some forty years ago, might have vied with many of the best establishments in London or Paris. Lord Normanby had a thousand good and amiable qualities; and those who knew him will long remember with regret his pleasant conversation, his genial smile, and kind, open-hearted manner.

A MOTHER IN ISRAEL.—Old Madame Rothschild, mother of the mighty capitalists, attained the age of ninety-eight; her wit, which was remarkable, and her intellectual faculties, which were of no common order, were preserved to the end. In her last illness, when surrounded by her family, her physician being present, she said in a suppliant tone to the latter, "Dear doctor, try to do something for me." "Madame, what can I do? I can't make you young again." "No, doctor, I don't want to be young again, but I want to continue to grow old."

EQUIPAGES IN LONDON AND PARIS—THE FOUR-IN-HAND CLUB.—When lately in London, on driving through the parks, I was struck with the inferiority of the equipages, to those which I remember fifty years ago. Paris now quite equals London in external display; indeed, the horses are, generally speaking, even superior. The Emperor, whose long residence in England gave him an opportunity of forming an idea of the care and attention necessary to produce a fine breed of horses, has been indefatigable in selecting a stud; and being ably seconded by General Fleury, introduced into France a love of sport which seemed almost peculiar to England.•

I look back upon the time when the most magnificent parade of horses and carriages attracted attention in London, and when the famous Four-in-hand Club was the theme of general admiration. The spectacle of a grand turn-out of the members of that distinguished body was one of the glories of the days of the Regent. There was a perfection in the minutest detail that made a well-appointed four-in-hand appear like a choice work of art. The symmetry of the horses, the arrangement of the harness, the plain but well-appointed carriage, the good taste of the liveries, the healthy, sturdy appearance of the coachmen and grooms, formed altogether one of those remarkable spectacles that make a lasting impression upon the memory.

The list of the members will shew that some of the most distinguished scions of the aristocracy were the persons who vied with each other in producing this effect. The original club embraced, I believe, the following leading members :—Lord Sefton, Lord Barrymore, Colonel Berkeley, afterwards Earl Fitzhardinge, Mr Akers, Sir Bellingham Graham, Sir Henry Peyton, Mr Clutterbuck, Mr Cholmondely of Vale Royal, Sir John Lade, Mr Lewis, Sir H. Mainwaring, Tom Richards, Mr Fenwick, Lord Worcester, Mr Rowles, and the Hon. Major Forrester. They assembled in George Street, Hanover Square, and drove in regular order to Salt Hill, to the well-known house, named the Windmill, kept by Botham, where a sumptuous dinner awaited them; after which they returned to London, in high spirits, and not unfrequently somewhat overcome by the quantity of sound port wine, for which that inn was celebrated.

The driving was never of such a character as to cause any accident; it was steady, and well regulated; one of the rules of the club being that no coach should pass another, and that the pace should never exceed a trot.

This club lasted in full vigour for upwards of twenty years, when it was broken up, in consequence of the death of many of the members, and the advanced age of several others. The love of coaching still existed amongst many distinguished leaders of fashion, and at a meeting held at the house of Lord Chesterfield, in Stanhope Street, it was determined to revive, in its former splendour, this national institution, which has served as an encouragement to the breeding of the finest cattle in the universe. Amongst my papers I found a list of the original members of this club, which met at Richmond on Saturday, June 2, 1838, and passed a series of resolutions, that formed the basis of the regulations which were observed during its existence.

The Earl of Sefton was one of the leaders of the

former club; he drove splendid bay horses, and was acknowledged to be a man of considerable taste. This noble Lord, with a frame somewhat deformed, was a capital horseman, and was seen daily in the parks, accompanied by his two daughters; one of whom had some pretensions to beauty, and married a son of the Whig member for Marlow, Pascoe Grenfell, a proprietor of copperworks at Swansea. Lord Sefton was amongst the most conspicuous lovers of the gastronomic art, and had secured Ude, the well-known *chef de cuisine* of Louis XVI. The noble Lord prided himself upon the invention of a famous *plat*, composed of the soft roe of the mackerel, which was served up in the form of *petits pâtés*.

Towards the end of his life, Lord Sefton became an *habitué* of Crockford's, and it was supposed that he left behind him there no less a sum than two hundred thousand pounds. After the death of the noble Lord, the fishmonger presented to his eldest son, who succeeded to the title, an acceptance of the late Lord's, to the tune of forty thousand pounds; and Lord Sefton, notwithstanding the uncertainty that attended a claim so abruptly made, felt it his duty to discharge the debt which he was led to believe had been incurred by his father.

The Marquis of Worcester, a spirited, dashing, handsome young man, was much admired by the fair sex, and led a life of great gaiety. His father, the Duke of Beaufort, receiving some hints that this promising youth was in danger of becoming the victim of a siren who had almost extorted from him a promise of marriage, the Marquis was sent to join the Duke of Wellington, became his aide-de-camp, and upon every occasion shewed that he was worthy the race of John of Gaunt, from which he sprang.

The lady in question (Harriet Wilson) was one of the most notorious *traviatas* of the day, had written her memoirs, and become the scandal of the metropolis; one of her sisters had married a peer of the realm, and another a famous harpist of very doubtful character, who had been one of the most licentious men of the day, and afterwards carried off the wife of a distinguished English composer.

Upon the return of the Marquis from the army, he devoted his time to the sports of the field, his father's hunting establishments, both in Gloucestershire and Oxfordshire, being the admiration of every lover of the chase. He married Miss Fitzroy, daughter of General and Lady Anne Fitzroy. Lady Anne, a sister of the Duke of Wellington, on the death of the General, became the wife of Sir Culling Smith. After the death of his beautiful wife, the Marquis of Worcester married her half-sister, from whom sprang the present Duke of Beaufort, who retains his ancestors' love of sport, and has lately made such a sensation in France by the splendid retinue he brought with him on the occasion of his visiting that country for the purpose of wolf-hunting. His late father was a universal favourite; a dandy of the first water, and very much beloved by all classes with whom he came in contact.

In the days of which I speak there were amateur coachmen, who drove with unflinching regularity, and in all weathers, the public stage-coaches, and delighted in the opportunity of assimilating themselves with professional Jehus. Some young men, heirs of large landed proprietors, mounted the box, handled the ribbons, and bowled along the high-road; they touched their hats to their passengers, and some among them did not disdain even the tip of a shilling or half-crown, with which it was the custom to remunerate the coachman. Many persons liked travelling to Brighton in "The Age," which was tooled along by Sir Vincent Cotton, whilst others preferred Charley Tyrrwhit. On the Holyhead, Oxford, and the Bath and Bristol roads, Lord Harborough, Lord Clonmel, Sir Thomas Mostyn, Sir Charles Bamfylde, Sir Felix Agar, Sir Henry Parnell, Sir Bellingham

Graham, Mr Clutterbuck, Sir John Lade, and other members of the Four-in-hand Club, were seen, either driving the coach or sitting cheek by jowl with the coachman, talking about horses and matters relating to "life upon the road." One of the members of the Four-in-hand Club, Mr Akers, was so determined to be looked upon as a regular coachman, that he had his front teeth so filed that a division between them might enable him to expel his spittle in the true fashion of some of the most knowing stage-coach drivers.

Lord Onslow devoted his time to his stud, and being the master of four of the finest black horses in England, was always conspicuous in the parks; but he was too eccentric to obtain the suffrages of any of the Four-in-hand Club, for his carriage was painted black, and the whole turn-out had more the appearance of belonging to an undertaker. Mrs Humphrey, at whose shop in St James's Street were exhibited all the best caricatures of the day, had a capital one in her window, in which the noble Lord was depicted driving his mournful equipage; and the following lines at the bottom were read with great glee by those who had seen the original:—

"What can Tommy Onslow do?
He can drive a curricle and two.
Can Tommy Onslow do no more?
Yes, he can drive a phaeton and four."

There was an individual once familiar in the dandy circle, whose turn-out made always a sensation from its excessive elegance, his name was Richards, but he acquired the cognomen of "Tom Pipes" from the following circumstance. Having run through an enormous fortune, he was compelled to borrow money at an exorbitant interest, and a well-known tobacconist in Oxford Street lent him large sums on the condition that Richards should take one-half of the amount in tobacco pipes, and other such commodities, and the needy man was always inviting his friends to take off his hands a portion of this stock in trade. He of course, like all other borrowers upon post-obit bonds, became completely ruined, and one kind friend obtained for him what in those days was a refuge of the destitute—a consulship. It was to Nantes he went; but his pecuniary difficulties hung about him, and he got into scrapes, and lost his appointment.

Richards had one redeeming point; he was a learned naturalist, and spent his little all in the purchase of animals. He got into trouble about a rare snake which he petted. Travelling in the Bath mail, he had placed the reptile in a basket under his feet; it crawled out and glided up the petticoat of a lady, who, suddenly waked up with an unusual sensation, pressed her hand upon the visitor, and irritated the snake, which gave her a severe bite.

Kate North.—In the days when "Skittles," "Anonyma," and other notorious descendants of the Laïses and Phrynes of old, are topics of conversation and newspaper comment, I may be permitted to "point a moral and adorn a tale," by relating a remarkable episode in the life and adventures of the beautiful and once celebrated Kate North.

Kate was the daughter of a discharged sergeant of the Guards, who had the appointment of sutler at Chatham. Her mother dying after a long illness, Kate, though young, worked hard early and late, and managed her father's house for a length of time; and the entire garrison, from the commanding officer to the private soldier, were loud in their praise of this incomparable young girl, whose marvellous beauty was the theme of conversation.

Among the officers at Chatham there happened to be a young ensign, extremely good-looking, upon whom Kate's beauty made a strong impression; he succeeded in captivating the affections of the charming and innocent girl, and at last seduced her. The regiment to which the ensign belonged having received marching orders, Kate determined to follow her seducer, and she marched with the soldiers to London. The secret of her seduction was not long before it got known and reached the ears of the Commander-in-Chief, the Duke of York; who, being informed that the poor girl was in a state of destitution, sent an aide-de-camp to discover her retreat, which proved to be an unfurnished room in the worst part of Spitalfields. The aide-de-camp told her his errand, but at the same time bound her to secrecy.

Early robbed of her virtue, abandoned by her betrayer, and an utter stranger in London, she reproached herself with her sin, and in a paroxysm of remorse and despair, the wretched girl determined to poison herself. She had purchased some laudanum, and was on the point of swallowing it, when a gentle rap at the door was heard outside. She opened the door, and in walked the Duke of York. His Royal Highness was struck with her beauty, modest deportment, and the frankness with which she answered all his questions, and, on his taking leave, said that he would send her a few necessaries to make her comfortable; upon which the poor girl fell upon her knees, and, in a voice almost inarticulate with emotion, thanked her benefactor.

When the Duke again called, she expressed her gratitude for all she had received, but hinted to her royal visitor that her earnest desire was to live an honourable life. The Duke was astounded, but said nothing in reply. He was simply dressed in a plain riding costume, and was, without exception, one of the finest men England could boast of. He stood above six feet; was rather stout, but well proportioned; his chest broad, and his frame muscular; his face bore the stamp of authority, and every feature was handsome; his brow was full and prominent, the eye grayish, beaming with benevolence; and a noble forehead, with premature gray hairs, though the Prince was hardly in the vale of years, completed the picture which presented itself to the unhappy Kate. The poor girl, overawed by the royal presence, attempted to leave the room, but was prevented. Her thoughts were how to avoid the danger which she felt was awaiting her, if the Royal Duke should persist in his assiduities.

His Royal Highness, not knowing the girl's feelings, paid her frequent visits, and each succeeding day became more and more enamoured of her; though upon all occasions she evinced a desire to avoid his presence. The thoughts of her seducer, and the degrading situation in which she stood, contrasting with the benevolence, and apparent affection of the Royal Duke, overwhelmed her. She wept bitterly, and flung herself upon her bed in an agony of distress. Her first resolution was to tell the Duke that she could not bring herself to consent to his proposals; but scarcely was the resolution formed, when the royal visitor again made his appearance. He promised never to desert her; and at length, overcome by his kindness and his importunities, she exclaimed, "If you really love me, Duke, I consent to be yours." The Duke was made happy; a house, carriages, &c., were supplied to the fair Kate, who lived with him many years. As she had a love for reading, and a desire for knowledge, masters were engaged for her; and by dint of perseverance, and applying herself to study, she was enabled to dissipate that weight of sorrow which would have otherwise hastened her death.

One summer morning a friend of the Duke of York's called and told her that His Royal Highness would be under the necessity of giving up his connexion with her, for he had promised the King, his father, that if his debts were paid, he would never more see the object of his affection. Poor Kate's heart was full; she could not reply to the messenger, but bursting into tears, hid her face, and flew out of the room. The sting which had been inflicted was more than she could bear, and she was seized with brain fever; but with much care and quiet, in course of time, the poor creature recovered her health and composure of mind.

There was no woman so much admired in London at the time as Kate North; her bewitching manners, the charm and grace of her conversation, brought to her pretty house in Green Street innumerable admirers. Among those anxious to woo her, a noble Scotch Lord was most assiduous in his attentions, and he at length succeeded in prevailing upon her to accept the offer of his protection; she lived with him several years, and bore him a daughter, who is now the wife of a baronet and the mother of a numerous family. But the canker in Kate's mind was all this while corroding her life. She visited Paris for change of air and scene; but there her senses left her: she became raving mad, and died in a foreign land, without a friend to close her eyes.

Sally Brooke.—There was a celebrated beauty who in my day made a conspicuous figure both in London and on the Continent. Miss Brooke, or as she was more generally called, Sally Brooke, was the daughter of a beneficed clergyman; she had agreeable manners, her education had been highly finished, and she always mingled in the best men's circles. For some reason which never was known, she quitted her parents' roof and came to London, where she created a considerable impression; she was most particularly noticed by the Prince of Wales, and consequently well received by those who basked in princely favour. Not a word, however, was ever breathed against her honour; and she was always looked upon as a model of unimpeachable veracity. Her beauty was such that she became the object of general admiration, and her portrait was taken by the first painters of the day. The Hebe by Strœling, engraved by Heath, remains to enable the world to form some idea of the matchless charms of the original. Her figure was perfection, and the sculptor would have been delighted to have obtained such a model. From whence she derived her income was always a mystery: a silly story was for a moment circulated that a person of the name of Bouverie, commonly called "The Commissioner," had succeeded in captivating her; this, however, soon died away. Whatever may have been her resources, she kept up a good establishment in Green Street, and lived always like a lady, but without much show. Her house was the rendezvous of the first men in London; but to her own sex she was distant and reserved, never admitting any female to her familiarity.

On one occasion, Miss Brooke dined at the house of a noble Marquis, where some of the fashionable young men of the day were invited to meet her; Mr Christopher Nugent, a nephew of the celebrated Burke, was most assiduous in his attentions, and begged permission to pay her a visit; the request was granted, and a day and an hour named. Some of the party present incidentally mentioned this engagement in the presence of the widow of a Mr Harrison, a lady who had access to the best circles in consequence of her remarkable beauty, and who had some right to place Mr Nugent on the list of her admirers. Jealous of her rival, the widow dressed herself as a boy, knocked at the door in Green Street, and was admitted into the presence of Miss Brooke, who was reclining on a sofa, whilst Nugent was on his knees before her; the distinguished lady, finding her lover in such a position, rushed upon him, seized a knife, and plunged it into his breast, fortunately without inflicting a mortal wound. Whatever might have been expected when this fact was generally known, it was soon believed that love had healed the wounds which jealousy inflicted; for Nugent and the lovely widow were soon seen walking together in familiar conversation in Hyde Park.

After being the admiration of the world of fashion for several seasons, Sally Brooke, seeing wrinkles coming into her once Hebe-like face, determined to leave scenes where she no longer reigned as the queen of beauty, but found other and fresher forms admired, and went to Baden. There some scoundrels having robbed her of all she possessed, she left the place, and arrived at the Hôtel du Palais Royal at Strasburg, where she remained some years, "the world forgetting, by the world forgot." A dropsical disease ravaged her once symmetrical form, and she died in a land of strangers. Her landlord nobly defrayed the expenses of her funeral, although she was already much indebted to him. Her family, however, liquidated her debts. Her remains repose in the city of Strasburg, and her tomb is one of the memorials of human vanity.

Madame Grassini.—One of the curious types of fifty years ago was the celebrated singer, Madame Grassini. When I first met her in 1825, she still possessed some remains of the remarkable beauty which had won for her the attention and admiration of so many of the great men of the age. Napoleon and Wellington, the Marshals of France, the Generals of the allied armies, English, Russians, Prussians, Austrians, as well as the Dukes and Marquises of the Restoration, had all bowed before Grassini's shrine, and had all been received with the same

Italian *bonhomie* and liberal kindness. She would often say, "Napoleon gave me this snuff-box; he placed it in my hands one morning when I had been to see him at the Tuileries, and added, 'Voilà pour toi; tu es une brave fille!' He was indeed a great man, but he would not follow my advice. Il aurait du s'entendre avec ce cher Vil-ainton. By the by, c'est ce brave Duc qui m'a donné cette broche. Il me la apporté un matin que j'étais encore au lit. Il parlait un singulier baragouin, et je ne savais guère l'Anglais; maïs nous nous entendions tout de même.' And so she would run on, with anecdotes and remarks on a long list of admirers.

All Madame Grassini's recollections came out quite naturally, with true southern frankness, or rather cynicism; and she narrated her *liaisons* in as unconcerned a manner before every one she met, as if she were speaking of her drive in the Bois de Boulogne. Her face must have been in her youth still handsomer than that of her niece, Giulia Grisi. The eyes were larger and more expressive, and she had more regular features and finer teeth. There was a tragic dignity in the contour and lineaments of her countenance, which formed a strange contrast with her unrefined language and gipsy style of dress; every colour of the rainbow was represented in her garments, which were tied on without the smallest regard to taste, and gave her very much the appearance of a strolling actress equipped at Ragfair.

Grassini's once fine voice had, when I saw her, degenerated into a sharp, loud, unmelodious soprano, which grated harshly on the ear. She had no cleverness or wit, and the *bons mots* that are cited as hers are amusing only from the cynic *bonhomie* which inspired them, as well as the strong Italian accent with which they were spoken. One of her *mots* in the days of the Empire is often cited. Napoleon had given the order of the Iron Crown to the famous castrato singer, Veluti, who was at that time all the fashion. This honour, at a period when decorations were given more sparingly than they are at present, created great discontent, especially amongst military men ; several of whom were complaining in no measured terms that the Lombard order should have been bestowed upon a mere singer, when Grassini interposed, with great vehemence, and said, "I am surprised that you soldiers should be so ungenerous, and not take into account *sa blessure.*"

I never shall forget the astonishment of Lord L——, some thirty-five years ago, when Grassini laid hold of him at a party at which I was present, and began relating to him her adventures with his father, "ce cher Charles S——." "Il vous ressemblait, Milord. Il n'était pas beau,—bien s'en faut; mais il était plus aimable que vous—il avait plus de grâce."

When Pasta first made her appearance, and the whole musical world was in an ecstasy of admiration, Grassini shrugged her shoulders, and exclaimed, "Ah, bah! si vous m'aviez entendu, c'était bien autre chose."

Madame Grassini was the possessor of a large fortune, and died in Paris at an advanced age.

Piety of Madame Catalani.—I knew the celebrated singer, Madame Catalani, when she lived in England. Her house was the rendezvous of many of the French *émigrés;* and as she was very rich and very generous, she frequently assisted those who were in the greatest distress. At the head of her profession, with the finest voice in the world, and the admired of all admirers, no whisper had ever been heard against her fair fame, and she lived in the utmost harmony with her husband, M. de Valabrèque. She was a most admirable woman in every relation of life, and as truly pious as she was kind and charitable.

An excellent friend of mine, Mr Fitzwilliam, so well known in Paris, informed me that as he was seated in the stage-box at the opera one night, when Madame Catalani was about to appear in one of her greatest parts, he observed her in the *coulisse*, before she had to come on, in an attitude of devotion, and evidently in earnest prayer, for the space of two or three minutes. When she had finished, she made the sign of the cross, and went on the stage, where, it is needless to say, she was received with unbounded applause. My friend, on calling upon the great singer next day, told her what he had observed; when she informed him, with a charming simplicity, that she never went upon the stage without first praying to God that He would grant her the favour to be enabled to sing well, and to meet with success; nor did she ever fail, on retiring to rest, to return thanks to Him for that and all the other mercies vouchsafed to her.

Miss T—— and the Perverts.—Dean Lockyer, a great favourite of George I., after a visit which he paid to Rome, was asked by His Majesty, in a jocular manner, as they sat over their bowl of punch, whether he had succeeded in converting the Pope. "No, your Majesty," replied the Dean; "His Holiness has most excellent Church preferment, and a most desirable bishopric, and I had nothing better to offer him." The same difficulties probably prevented the success of Miss T——, an excellent young Scotch lady, who went to Rome some years ago with the express purpose of converting to Presbyterianism the great head of the Roman Catholic Church. Miss T——, instead of succeeding in her object, was herself converted, or perverted, to Catholicism, and is at this moment superior of a convent at Edinburgh.

When I was last at Rome I was much disgusted at the absurd over-zeal of the English perverts, who were first and foremost in every procession, prostrating themselves on the saliva-covered floor of the churches before the most grotesque idols or absurd relics, and kissing, with a display of the most ardent devotion, St Peter's well-worn toe, just after the same ceremony had been performed by some filthy Trasteverine reeking of garlic and covered with vermin. It used to be said, at the time of the Restoration in 1815, that many of the followers of Louis XVIII. were more *royalistes que le roi ;* and the same saying may be applied to our vulgar English perverts, who are more Popish than the Pope, and make themselves the laughing-stock of Antonelli, and the great majority of cardinals and abbés, who believe in nothing at all.

RACHEL'S DÉBUT.—When the inimitable Rachel

first appeared at the Théâtre Français, M. Prevost, secretary of the theatre, and well known for his good taste and judgment in all theatrical matters, was accosted by the young *débutante*, begging him to give her a few lessons in declamation. Prevost, surprised at this request, replied, "Ma pauvre fille, allez vendre des bouquets." Soon after this Rachel appeared for the first time in "Hermione." Her acting electrified the audience, and on the fall of the curtain bouquets were thrown to her from nearly every box in the theatre. She modestly courtesied, and picked them up; then, taking them to Prevost, she said, "I have followed your advice, and bring you the bouquets for sale." Upon which the secretary fell upon his knees before the great *tragédienne*, acknowledging his haste and rudeness, and expressing regret for having wounded the feelings of the *débutante*.

RACHEL AND JUDITH.—Mademoiselle Judith, the clever and accomplished actress of the Théâtre Français, was one day abusing, in no measured terms, her fellow-*tragédienne*, Mademoiselle Rachel, to a mutual friend, the celebrated Doctor D——. After expatiating upon her many faults, and, above all, her grasping rapacity, she wound up by saying, "C'est une vraie Juive." The doctor, somewhat surprised, said, "Surely, my dear Judith, that ought not to be a fault in your eyes; as you likewise belong to the same religious persuasion." "True," replied the witty actress; "but the difference is, that I am a Jewess, and she is a Jew."

This reminds me of a late saying of James Rothschild's, who, furious at the encreasing prosperity of his rival, Pereire, exclaimed, with the same forgetfulness of their mutual nationality, "How can anybody transact business with such a wretched little Jew?"

ROSSINI.—Rossini has been for some time a resident in Paris; and whenever he receives, every one is anxious to be admitted to his soirees, where good music is sure to be heard, or to his dinner-table, where excellent macaroni is as certain to be served up. The master looks in perfect health, and has more of the Englishman than the Italian in his personal appearance. The photographs that are sold of him are perfect of their kind, and express the good-nature and sly humour for which he is remarkable. He lives a large portion of the year at Passy, where the Parisian municipality made him a present of the ground upon which he has built his villa in the Italian style.

Rossini narrates, at his dinner parties, with great

glee, some of the circumstances that occurred to him in London. He was made a great deal of by the Prince Regent; and on one occasion he could not help shewing how little pleasure he derived from the attempts made by His Royal Highness to execute some passages, in which he totally failed owing to his inability to keep time: for the Regent, though a great lover of music, and not a bad player on the violin, constantly put out the *maestro*, to whom he at last offered an apology. Rossini accepted it with civility, and good-naturedly said, "There are few in your Royal Highness's position who could play so well."

Rossini was not aware of a law which then existed, by which a foreigner might be imprisoned for debt without any warning, and merely upon the affidavit of a creditor affirming that the stranger was about to leave England. He was once arrested in London by a bailiff, and carried to a sponging-house, and though his incarceration was of short duration, it gave him a disgust for a city where he had otherwise been well received.

Rossini does not go as often to the opera as might be expected, preferring the agreeable society of a few friends. He has also a strong objection to go out to parties; even the Emperor's invitations have no weight with him, and he has frequently begged to be excused. Rossini is an enemy to modern innovations, and has never yet trusted himself to the railroad. No inducement could be found sufficiently strong for him to travel otherwise than in a coach drawn by horses, and that at so moderate a speed, that a week was occupied by him in his journey from Paris to Baden.

Madame Colbrand, the *prima donna* at Naples when Rossini commenced his career as a composer, exercised considerable influence on the success of his earliest operas. They were written expressly for her, at a period when the heyday of her youth was gone by, she having long been an acknowledged favourite both with the manager and King Ferdinand. When "Elisabetta" was produced in 1815 by the young *maestro,* Madame Colbrand retained all the beauty of her voice, which, added to her physical advantages and a commanding figure, fine features, and dignified bearing, called forth a shout of applause as she appeared on the stage of San Carlo, in the character of the English queen. The duet with Leicester secured the success of this the first opera that Rossini had produced at Naples, and others which followed in quick succession were received with the enthusiastic admiration they so fully merited.

But it was reserved for that unrivalled *artiste,* Madame Pasta, to come up to the full exigencies of

Rossini's musical genius. Her appearance at Her Majesty's Theatre electrified the house; and none who are old enough to remember the great *Diva*, can forget the wonderful pathos and power of that rich-toned thrilling voice, whose somewhat husky notes seemed to deepen the effect of her singing upon the hearts of her auditors.

To descend from grave to gay, I remember hearing one of her ardent admirers at that time, when Pasta, having just come off the stage, was refreshing herself, asking her, in his most romantic tones, "Signora, prendete limonata o sorbetto?" "No," answered the great singer in her deep voice; "prendo 'af-an'-'af [half-and-half] adesso."

Pio Nono's Flight to Gaeta.—All who are personally acquainted with Pope Pius IX. are aware that he is a man of extremely benevolent disposition, naturally liberal in his political views, and desirous of promoting the welfare and happiness of mankind. Political events in 1847-48, were singularly calculated to bring out the peculiar characteristics of a sovereign Pontiff who was called upon to exercise his temporal power in an exceptional period of modern Italian history. Pius IX. believed that it was not incompatible with the attributes of the Papacy, to participate in that great liberal movement which shook so many thrones in the year 1848. The College of Cardinals, and especially the conspicuous members of the order of the Jesuits, became alarmed at the Pontiff's liberal ideas. Knowing well his character, and observing the progress of that overwhelming tide of popular opinion which was sweeping sovereigns from their thrones, and shaking the very foundations of government, they did not at first openly oppose the Pontiff's views, but gradually and insidiously set about creating alarm in his mind, and above all, sought to awaken doubts in the conscience of "the Vicar of Christ." They calculated, and correctly, that if they could not deter him from bestowing mundane and political benefits on the Roman people, they could at least make him believe that in doing so he was betraying the interests and influences of the Catholic Church, and they succeeded in arousing a tempest of indignation and alarm in the mind of Pio Nono, until he felt it his duty to take to flight, more in the cause of the Roman Catholic Church than from fears concerning personal safety.

The golden tints of an Italian sunset had faded into that brief twilight which heralds darkness, when a female, dressed in humble attire, was admitted to the garden of the Vatican by a gentleman in the confidence of the Pope. Neither of the persons spoke as they made their way to a portion of the palace not generally inhabited. On arriving at the foot of a dark and narrow staircase, the gentleman took from his pocket one of those little knots of twisted wax-taper which the Italians carry about with them, and lighted it; then, without uttering a word, he beckoned the lady to follow him, and proceeded up the narrow stone staircase, which, after many windings, led to a door, on which three raps were given by the mysterious guide. Almost immediately the door was opened by Pio Nono himself, and the guide, making way for the lady, retired. This was Madame Dodwell, to whom I alluded in my second volume as one of the most beautiful women of her time; she was the widow of an Englishman, though a Roman by birth, and married *en secondes noces* to the Bavarian minister, and she had come to the Vatican in order to arrange the clandestine flight of the Pontiff from Rome.

His Holiness appeared to have lost all presence of mind, and trembled as he took the lady by the hand, and gazing earnestly on her still beautiful face, said, "I look to you, madam, for arranging all details. I have the utmost confidence in your discretion, and I know the firmness of your character." The lady replied, "Has any plan of escape suggested itself to your Holiness?" "Yes," said the Pontiff in a low voice; "I think the best thing I can do is to put on the gown of an ordinary priest, and at daybreak to-morrow morning walk out of the gates which conduct to the Fondi road. You, madam, in your carriage, will have preceded me, and, waiting at a convenient distance, you will take me up. I have made arrangements with my good and faithful friend, Ferdinand, King of Naples, for a safe retreat at Gaeta; and I have no doubt that you, with your passport as Ambassadress of Bavaria, can pass the customs authorities with little or no difficulty." "Holy father," replied the lady, pressing the Pontiff's hand, "the scheme seems to me in every way satisfactory. I shall bring with me a confidential servant, a clever coachman, willing to brave any danger." The Pope rose, and bestowing his blessing on the lady, ushered her to the door, adding, "I retire to pass the night in prayer.' "I shall be one mile from the gate on the Fondi road," said the lady in a whisper, "by four o'clock to-morrow morning."

At that hour a carriage might have been seen in a bend of the road which leads to Naples. On the box-seat beside the coachman sat a female, dressed as a domestic servant, who anxiously gazed around while waiting the arrival of the Pope. She did not wait long before she beheld approaching a thick-set and somewhat corpulent priest, who advanced towards the carriage with a rapid step, and covered with dust. In a few minutes Pio Nono was seated in the carriage with the ambassadress, and the horses were whipped into a gallop, and did not halt until they reached the small customhouse of Fondi.

It was now ten o'clock, and they were immediately surrounded by the customhouse officers, who demanded their passports. The chief official, looking into the carriage, observed, "I do not find on your passport the name of the priest who accompanies your excellency." "Oh," replied the lady, "he is only my confessor." Unfortunately, the priest shewed signs of uneasiness and alarm, which excited the suspicion of the officer, who said, "In these times our orders are very strict, and I cannot permit the *padre confessore* to pass. I must beg him to descend, and shall be obliged to detain him until I get permission from Rome for his release." The Pope, hearing this, was in a great state of excitement; he caught hold of the man's hand, and whispered in his ear, "*Caro amico,* you don't know who I am,—I am your sovereign and father, Pius IX." Whereupon the officer turned round to a little group of persons who had collected, and exclaimed, "Per Baccho, here is a fellow who calls himself our Pope!" The crowd peered into the carriage, and indulged in a volley of ribaldry, evidently not believing in the identity of the sovereign Pontiff. Matters were becoming serious, when the Pope placed a bag of gold coin in the hands of the officials, whilst the ambassadress threw handfuls of scudi to the mob. A loud cheer was raised by all present, and in a few minutes the carriage was going at full speed, without fear of pursuit, on the road to Gaeta.

SUDDEN TURNS OF FORTUNE IN FRANCE.—I have seen some of those marvellous changes in France which have made all Europe wonder. Kings, statesmen, financiers, marshals, ambassadors, and ministers of state, have risen up and faded away before my eyes. An empire, an army, a city, have risen from the old foundations, through the debris of a revolutionary government. How long the present state of things is to last, no human foresight can tell. A *coup d'état* has once succeeded; why may not another? One army has left its much-loved sovereign; why not another? Every one believed that Charles X. was popular with the army; the Gardes du Corps and the Garde Royale seemed ready to lay down their lives in his defence; and only a few days before the revolution of July, no one had the slightest doubt that every soldier was prepared to do his duty whenever called upon. Yet how few accompanied the fallen monarch on his way to embarkation for a foreign land.

Men who are now playing an active part in life, and occupying a great position, I have known in very different circumstances, apparently not possessing the means of elevating themselves to a higher grade in society. For instance, one of the great men near the Emperor was, prior to the revolution, obliged to have recourse to the editorship of a journal, *Le Messager du Soir,* in conjunction with his friend Monsieur Brindeau, a person employed at the Bourse. A late French ambassador, whose name has so lately been before the public in connexion with the march of affairs in Italy, filled a very humble position when I was first made known to him; he was then only a clerk at a small bank in the Rue Lafitte, kept by Messrs Orr & Goldsmith, which, with many others in Paris, has vanished. My friend married a daughter of a rich London distiller.

The last revolution, no doubt, brought down some substantial houses, as it cleared away some of doubtful character. Messrs —— & —— retired upon that occasion; but they have, however, again commenced separately. The railroad to Boulogne was under the auspices of that firm; but it has now become a part of the Great Northern line. The Rouen Railway also aided Messrs —— & —— in regaining their lost money, though many of the original subscribers were unfortunately ruined; and the separation of the two partners of the firm appears to have been attended with good results to both, judging from the external appearance of wealth exhibited in their magnificent hotels, their splendid equipages, their powdered lackeys, and their luxurious style of living.

True, the most solid and established houses do not follow the example set by some of the moneyed gentry. Few establishments maintain such a high reputation as the old and respected firm of Mallet, whose name is associated with worth, economy, and good sense, and where everything is straightforward and honourable. They have no box at the Grand Opera, or at the Italiens, for their families, who do not seek, by gorgeous promenades in the Bois de Boulogne, to dazzle the eyes of the poor, and outvie the *demi monde* in insolence and extravagance; creating envy and dissatisfaction in those who may have suffered from the failure of other establishments. Indeed some of the financiers of the day have been of great public service, and their honoured names are not to be associated with those who have played a game disreputable to themselves, and injurious to their fellow-citizens.

Messrs Rothschild and Pereire—who may not like to see their names in the same paragraph, as it is generally believed that they are by no means on good terms with each other—are amongst the leading moneyed men of the day, and both of them have been of service to the state. The Rothschilds have the credit of being very liberal to those who require their aid, although by no means allowing themselves to be imposed upon by the solicitations of the idle and dissolute. Many acts of kindness are related of them; and they are known to be generous in their hospitality, and charitable to the stranger. M. Pereire, who was once a clerk in the house of Rothschild, has made a rapid fortune, and has acquired a high reputation as a financier, by founding that successful institution, "The Credit Mobilier;" and he has many warm friends, who speak highly of his liberality and disinterestedness. He has built a splendid hotel near the British Embassy, and furnished it with artistic taste, and there he receives his friends with splendid hospitality.

Parisian Cockneydom.—Although I entertain a high opinion of the Parisians and Frenchmen generally, I believe that there is no human being more thoroughly ignorant and conceited than the uneducated Parisian Cockney or *badaud.* Of other countries he has scarcely any knowledge ; and he is firmly convinced that the French are the masters of the world, and that no people on the face of the earth can enter into competition with them in war, literature, arts, or science : perfection is only to be found in his native land. He turns up his nose contemptuously at everything English ; all his notions of England being derived from the low theatres on the Boulevards, where British, Russian, Austrian, and Prussian soldiers are invariably put *hors de combat* by the French. He is very fond of talking of an invasion of the "Little Island," and fully believes that sooner or later a Zouave will be "Duke of London," and some *employé* of the French Government, "Prefect of the Thames." He is firmly convinced that the English visitors come to Paris only to be astonished at the magnificent edifices of the city, to gaze at the Louvre and the beautiful monuments; though the great attraction to them is, in his opinion, the good dinners that are to be eaten in Paris, for he thinks that there is nothing in London to tempt the appetite but half-raw beef. As for fresh vegetables, sauce for fish, and good pastry, nothing of the sort is to be obtained there, and a French beggar would disdain to partake of the meals which the ravenous Londoner devours. But when John Bull comes to Paris, the beautiful metropolis of France,—of Europe,—he finds apartments to lodge in superior even to those which the Queen occupies at Buckingham Palace or Windsor Castle, at a moderate price, while his table is served with a luxury nowhere else to be found.

Louis Philippe committed a great mistake, and caused much mischief, by his patronage of the *bourgeoisie,* who not only introduced vulgar manners, but conducted themselves with great insolence; aping, as far as they could, the style of persons of good blood and high rank and station. Unfortunately, the revolution of 1830 had overthrown the fortunes of one half of the aristocratic families, who were consequently compelled to shut up their hotels, discharge their servants, and retire from the world. Since that period the domestics have imitated their masters in their follies, and flaunt themselves in silk dresses and expensive bonnets, instead of the pretty muslin caps and modest dimity gowns which formerly became the *bonnes* and cook-maids. Wages necessarily became doubled; nay, even tripled; the tradesmen connived with the servants to plunder the family, and extravagance became the order of the day. Paris has rapidly increased in size, and the idle and dissolute have consequently congregated in this overgrown city. But, alas! it also became the rendezvous of all the miscreants that other great cities have expelled: here are to be found the liberated convict and the depraved harlot, rioting in luxury, and offending the eyes of modesty and rectitude. It is calculated that the population now exceeds 1,500,000 souls, and to preserve order, and give security to the honest portion of the inhabitants, it is necessary that 40,000 police should be kept in constant employment.

I cannot refrain from alluding also to the extortionate prices which, I regret to say, my fellow-countrymen are compelled to pay for every article they require. There is a league amongst the shopkeepers, the proprietors of hotels, the restaurateurs, and even the humble porter whose occupation it is to stand at the corner of the street; they have one common interest, which is to extract from the pockets of John Bull whatever money they can extort from him on any pretext.

The large and magnificent shops in the Rue de la Paix, in the Rue Castigleone, in the Faubourg St Honoré, and the Rue de Rivoli, are sources of immense wealth; and it is a well-known fact that, in the course of six years, tradesmen who occupy them accumulate large fortunes, and are enabled to retire from business. Should a war occur between France and England, all those splendid establishments would be closed; for it is chiefly on the money spent by foreigners, and more especially by the English, that Paris tradesmen subsist. If the Duchesse d'Abrantes, whose Memoirs were so universally read during the Restoration, had been alive at the present time, she would have been horrified at the marvellous change for the worse that has taken place. The Duchess, who was evidently a person of enlarged mind, and fully alive to the iniquities of this wicked world, says in one of her volumes that there is not a more industrious class of persons than the artisans of Paris, who toil eighteen hours out of the twenty-four, and carry to the shopkeeper the produce of their labour; and, by dint of coaxing and entreaty, induce him to give enough to keep their body and soul together; immediately after, the extortionate shopkeeper obtains from some of his customers a price equal to a profit of five hundred per cent. This system prevails in every department; the industrious peasant who brings to the market the produce of his garden, is compelled by the municipal authorities to sell at the Halle, (the great market,) before seven in the morning, whatever he has brought. If he does not find customers, he is quickly surrounded by innumerable harpies, who induce the hard-working labourer to sell to them his vegetables and fruit at less than half their value. These harpies are themselves small vendors of these articles, and I do not hesitate to affirm that they realise a profit of four hundred per cent. on their bargains. Then the wine-merchant, who purchases his wines at Bordeaux or Maçon, or the borders of the Rhone, generally receives a genuine and pure produce of the grape; but when this wine is brought to market in Paris, it has marvellously increased in bulk, for *every* cask of real wine is, by the aid of water and logwood, converted into three, and sold as genuine wine.

A celebrated surgeon, a resident of the Faubourg St Germain, related to me the following fact. He accepted an invitation to dine at the house of a well-known nobleman, distinguished in the fashionable world. The dinner was all that the most delicate taste could offer; the *cuisine* was inimitable, the wines of the choicest *cru*, the dessert rich and tempting. Several of the *plats* left the table untouched; the doctor observed that pine apples and grapes were abundant, and that so plentiful was the supply, that many plates were taken from the table exactly as they were placed upon it. The dinner being over, the gentlemen and ladies retired to the *salon,* and they had scarcely entered it, when a relation of the Amphitryon's unexpectedly arrived, after a long journey, from the provinces. He was received with the utmost cordiality by the family, and was naturally asked if he had dined; on his reply in the negative, that in fact he had tasted nothing since he left Lyons, the bell was rung, and the servant ordered to prepare something for the hungry traveller. The servant shortly returned to the *salon,* and, to the inexpressible astonishment of every one present, said that the *maître d'hôtel* had desired him to say that there was nothing left; on the *maître d'hôtel* being questioned, he confirmed the statement of the domestic, whereupon he immediately received from his indignant master orders to quit his service in twelve hours. On receiving his ill-gained wages, the man acknowledged that he had disposed of the dinner amongst his fellow-servants, as he considered that every article became his property, with the exception of the dessert, which belonged to Chevet of the Palais Royal, who farmed out the fruit and sweets that composed it at a certain sum per dinner.

The porters, or, as they now denominate themselves, the *concierges,* are perhaps the worst species of servants that ever infested a domestic establishment. They are inadequately paid by the proprietor, and consequently prey upon those who have the misfortune of living under their surveillance. In fact they are rogues and thieves in disguise: they compel the tradesmen who serve those who live in the house to pay five per cent. for every article that enters; wine, wood, coal, and indeed almost every article, is subject to this abominable mode of levying contributions from the residents.

Improvements in Paris.—Paris has within four or five years undergone marvellous changes, which reflect the highest honour on those who have contributed to its splendour at the present time. The melancholy, gloomy, miserable portion of the city might be very charming to the artist and archæologist, who admired mediæval pointed roofs, fantastic domes, labyrinths of galleries, and windows that seemed as if not intended to admit the air or the sunlight; whilst liquid mud and filthy streams sluggishly meandered through the dark and narrow streets and passages, from which the frightened foreigner could scarcely extricate himself. A beautiful, fairy-like city has replaced the crowded heaps of dingy, dark dwellings; the blind alleys and the fetid courts have been exchanged for lofty and elegant mansions, wide and well-paved thoroughfares, and spacious open places. A writer of antiquity denominated Paris *Leukotokia*, the white city. Well now does it merit that name. All that was may have been picturesque; but all that is must be pronounced delightful. We may have lost the identical spot where the body of Admiral Coligny fell on St Bartholomew's day; we may inquire after the street through which passed the carriage where sat the good and glorious Henri of Navarre, when he was assassinated by Ravaillac; the narrow street has also disappeared where the assassins lurked with an infernal machine to blow up the First Consul. But upon sites once covered with cemeteries, with sewers, with pits, and with abominations indescribable, have arisen verdant lawns, squares, and gardens, where, at the vernal season, flowers charm the eye and gratify the sense, while sparkling fountains pour forth their cool streams; spaces where the sun and air give life and animation to all around; mansions where domestic or polished society can enjoy all the luxuries and comforts which art and taste have introduced.

This transformation has been effected at an enormous expense, by skilful architects and sculptors, under the control of one great sovereign; it has been the result of unremitting energy on the part of those who planned the improvements, and the indomitable toil of those who carried them out.

It was indeed a sight worthy this engineering age, to see the thousand workmen congregated upon various spots, the tram-roads, and trains of horses and waggons bearing enormous weights of stone from the neighbouring quarries, the crumbling houses marked for destruction, and the deep foundations dug for new Boulevards on both banks of the Seine, the delight of Paris. Palaces have sprung up, which may give historic recollections to future generations quite as interesting as those we have received from the Tour de Nesle, where a queen carried on her licentious intrigues ; or as the Hôtel de Sens, and the Hôtel des Tournelles, the residence of princes, where bravoes issued forth to murder, and in whose dungeons languished the good and the brave, as well as the criminal ; or the convents of the Cordeliers, the Benedictines, and the thousand lazy monks of the olden time. One of the most glorious achievements of the present reign has been the completion of that magnificent edifice, the Louvre. Its saloons, lined with treasures of fine art, were the glory of France ; but a large portion of this vast structure, only a very short time ago, wore a most ignoble aspect : columns, with rich capitals, were at their base disfigured by all that was filthy and disgusting. The square that had displayed the talents of Jean Goujon, and of

Perrault,—where Catherine de Medicis and her sons, where Henry IV. and Margot, gazed from the windows,—adjoined stalls where squalid people offered for sale dogs, birds, the sweepings of *bric-à-brac* shops; spots infested by the lazzaroni of Paris, thieves, and courtesans. A more painful contrast of luxury and misery never disfigured the most attractive part of a luxurious city. Napoleon I., in the plenitude of his power, and Louis Philippe, with all the *bourgeoisie* of Paris to back him, could not drive away the human vermin that infested the place; nor did they add a single stone to improve this *chef d'œuvre* of architecture. At length, to the immortal honour of the Emperor Napoleon III., the work has been accomplished, and the Louvre is now a palace worthy of the *chefs d'œuvres* of art, which enrich its interior. Indeed, the inauguration of the Louvre is an era in the annals of Paris.

The cleansing, draining, and lighting of the streets have also been admirably carried out; and the famous city of Paris now appears with renovated grace and beauty, and decorated with a thousand ornaments, which attract the eyes of the whole world. There has been another immense improvement: the groves of the Bois de Boulogne, formerly the rendezvous of duellists, footpads, and gipsies, have been transformed as if by the hand of an enchanter, and flowers and foliage, velvet turf, cascades, and winding streams combine to delight the senses and invigorate the health of the promenaders. Here lovers, idlers, poets, the humble and the wealthy, lounge their hours away amid joyous scenes, where art and skill have successfully combined the varied charms of nature.

French Criminal Jurisprudence.—A trial for a criminal offence is one of the most remarkable scenes that France affords. In every respect it essentially differs from what occurs in England, and produces a sensation of disgust amongst those who have witnessed an offender arraigned in the British Isles. A feeling of sympathy is there entertained for the prisoner at the bar, whom the law assumes to be innocent until he is proved guilty. Seldom is any emotion exhibited, or if there be any, it is mostly in favour of the prisoner. Far different is the case in a French court of justice. An unfortunate being seems to be set up to be mentally tortured; every effort is made by the judge and by the *procureur-général* to convict him out of his own mouth; he is cross-questioned, brow-beaten, and every device is employed to entrap him into a confession. He has most probably been confined for months previously on suspicion, and during that time has been cross-examined, entreated, and persuaded by a *iuge d'instruction* to acknowledge himself guilty. Enfeebled in body by long confinement, and harassed in mind, he is called upon, before an excitable auditory, to combat with highly-educated legal opponents, who watch with unwearied vigilance every change of countenance, every expression of emotion, listen with eager anxiety to any faltering of the voice or hesitation of speech, and seem to rejoice if, by accumulation of evidence, they can fix upon him the stigma of crime. He has no protection from either judge, jury, or prosecutors; he is interrogated, not with a view of ascertaining the truth, much less of proving innocence, but in order to prove him guilty. The spectators, in a state of excitement, watching with eager curiosity every phase of the scene acting before them, do not disguise their emotions; compassion, horror, disgust, vengeance, and other passions are awakened and expressed openly, often with the purpose of producing an effect upon the judge and jury.

The criminal process in France will probably be somewhat improved, and imprisonment before trial will then be no longer enforced; for the highest legal authorities are occupied with the endeavour to alleviate some of the worst features of French criminal trials: indeed it is generally understood that the Emperor will soon sign a decree prepared by the Minister of Justice, which will modify the existing practice, and that the system of finding bail, which has so long existed in England, will be substituted for preliminary imprisonment.

The banker Mires was long confined in prison before trial, and afterwards his innocence was established by a jury. In a recent notorious trial, where a rich landed proprietor at Marseilles was accused of attempting to murder his servant, the accused suffered eight months' imprisonment before he was brought to trial, and then was pronounced not guilty; but he had no redress for this long and painful incarceration. The eminent men now at the French bar are for the most part anxious for an amelioration of this and other defects in the *Code Napoléon.*

Some of the leading advocates take an active part in politics, and for the most part belong to the Liberal party. M. de Berryer, however, one of the most eloquent men of the day, and who defended Prince Louis Napoleon after the memorable affair at Boulogne, is an acknowledged and stanch Royalist; he supports the claims of the Comte de Chambord, who very wisely says, "I will come to you, if you want me, and send for me; but otherwise, I intend remaining quietly at Frohsdorff. A crown has no great charms for me; and if I put yours upon my head, Frenchmen may some time or other wish to take it off, and very possibly my head at the same time." What the politics of M. Dupin may be, now or hereafter, nobody can well guess. He was once a stanch Orleanist, then a confirmed Republican, and is now a lukewarm Napoleonist. M. Marie, an accomplished orator, remains a Republican: he became a member of the Provisional Government, but was somewhat timid; always fearing some excess upon the part of the people. M. Cremieux, one of the ugliest little men that France can boast of, seems to have retired from political life: energetic, even violent in action when speaking, he is a sound lawyer and an able advocate.

M. Jules Favre is a great favourite; an acute and intellectual pleader, he is employed by all parties; but his ultra-liberal views are not always relished. He is a fluent speaker, and has the tact of making juries attentive to him; for he has a plain, straightforward manner of speaking, and his language is pure and correct. None of the first men at the bar at the present day have been remarkable for literary success; in fact it would appear that literary pursuits are considered almost incompatible with legal distinction. There is an Englishman, a Mr Jones, practising with some success at the French bar. But there is a striking difference in many points from the practice of the law of England, which renders any approximation of the courts of the two countries quite out of the question.

There is an idea in France that French literature is predominant throughout the whole of Europe; and it is the firm belief of the mass of the French people that their authors of the present day take precedence over all others. Undoubtedly French dramas and novels have lately found favour in England: Victor Hugo, Alexandre Dumas, Madame George Sand, have found translators of their more striking romances; but their historians, philosophers, and moralists are much less known and esteemed abroad than those of Germany; indeed, the German language is beginning to be studied by thinking men and women with much more assiduity than the French. French plays, adapted to the English stage, have of late years been more popular in England than the Shakspearean drama; but literary revolutions are of such frequent and rapid occurrence, that the caprice of to-day may be forgotten to-morrow. Dramas of political intrigues are now the order of the day in Paris; will they be transferred to the London boards?

Every one in France is looking to the effect that

will be produced by free trade in dramatic literature; importations from England will probably be more frequent, as the censorship has generally exerted its influence to prevent the stage offering a representation of the manners and customs of the British, and has weighed heavily upon authors and managers. Freed from the tyranny that has confined the human mind to a certain class of ideas, new dramatists will arise, and we shall have fresh subjects brought on the French stage; genuine comedy may then assert her powers of depicting "the living manners as they rise."

The Paris Insurrection of 1848.—No one, who now for the first time visits Paris, can comprehend how such a magnificent city could be converted into a strong fortress, with impediments to the action of the military on every side. The magnificent, broad, and well-macadamised streets, through which successive regiments and parks of artillery can move without dread of molestation, seem little adapted for *émeutes* and barricades. But far different was the aspect a few years since. Narrow, close, confined streets, paved with huge stones, were alone to be seen; and there were quarters of the town inhabited by a desperate and poor population, in a state of squalid misery, and ever ready to fly to arms and raise barricades at the summons of a few political fanatics. When an opposition to the existing government was decided upon by a few active demagogues, there poured forth, from dens of darkness and abodes of filth, a mass of people who at other periods scarcely ever saw daylight, and who wildly expected to lessen their sufferings and improve their condition by acts of violence. No one had attempted to ameliorate their condition ; it was not dreamt that, by the judicious expenditure of money, these people might be made good citizens, and enabled to throw off the yoke of crime and misery. Yet, in a few short years, a marvellous change has come over the spirit of the "dangerous classes." The spots where they congregated are covered with lofty mansions, and the former inhabitants have migrated to less densely-populated districts, and are able to obtain honest employment. The Faubourg St Antoine, the Barrière du Trône, and the environs are no longer under the control of two or three fiery demagogues, but have become the quiet habitations of a class that has learnt to respect itself.

When, in former days, an *émeute* was decided upon, it was the result of much previous deliberation by the leading members of secret clubs, who planned a strategic movement, which they induced a number of ill-fed, ill-conditioned, discontented, and reckless men to carry out. Their object was to impede the march of troops, by the erection of barricades; to take possession of the neighbouring houses, and from the windows hurl missiles of every description upon their opponents. From the Batignolles in the north, from St Antoine in the east, and from the Quartier Latin in the south, there simultaneously poured forth hosts of the humbler class; their great object being to meet near the Hôtel de Ville, and, gaining possession of it, to form a provisional government, and issue thence proclamations.

In 1848, Louis Philippe's government succumbed to the manœuvres of the insurgents; but when, at a later period, General Cavaignac made up his mind to support the Legislative Assembly, the tables were turned. The battle, however, was most sanguinary—the resistance desperate. In a few hours rose up, as if by the labour of Cyclopeans, masses of stone gathered from the paved streets, which seemed to defy all attempts to overthrow them; and behind these barricades stood resolute and excited men, armed with every species of offensive weapon, vociferating defiance and contempt of those who attempted to dislodge them; while every house in the neighbourhood became an arsenal of deadly missiles. The insurgents would have gained the victory had their opponents not sprung from their own ranks; for the soldiery were little inclined to act. But the National Guard, upon whom rested almost the whole of the encounter, had fortunately been recruited by many of the very men who had joined the insurrection in the previous February. Lamartine and his colleagues had, with great prudence, and more judgment than they usually exhibited, enlisted, in some regiments to which they gave the name of "La Garde Mobile," all the idle young men and *gamins* of Paris who had taken up arms on the former occasion. Animated by a love of the service they had so lately joined, and controlled by military discipline, they forgot that they were firing upon their friends and relations; and, being boldly led on, they executed their task with devotion and courage. Dreadful was the carnage and devastation: the next day the Faubourg St Antoine and the neighbourhood of the Bastille presented the appearance of a city taken by storm.

General Cavaignac had not been sparing in his chastisement of the people, and a vivid recollection of the punishment he had inflicted was long preserved. But no beneficial results followed this terrible battle; for the Legislative Assembly were satisfied with having thus made an example of the misguided, and strengthened their own power.

With the usual heedlessness of the Parisians, the whole affair was nearly forgotten in a few weeks, and the lives that had been lost were scarcely thought of. Eleven generals had been either killed or wounded, and the slaughter had been tremendous; but it produced no permanent effect: no effort was made to prevent future risings. Red-republicanism, it is true, had received a severe blow; but nothing was done to alleviate the sufferings, or enlighten the understandings of the people; nor was the good feeling of the nation appealed to. Indeed, excepting in two or three of the *soi-disant* Liberal journals, no narrative of the fatal events was published; for a great struggle for power was then going on amongst the different parties. Legitimists, Orleanists, and Liberals were only occupied in calculating their strength in the Chamber; and aspiring individuals indulged in hopes that the party to which they looked for their own advancement would triumph.

French Statesmen and Journalists in 1851.—Ever since my first visit to Paris in 1815, there has been political agitation in France; unfortunately not that of statesmen, but that of ambitious men, each one anxious to fill the highest office in the state, for which every one here thinks he has sufficient capacity. The doctrine that the humblest may rise to the highest rank is well adapted for the army, where personal courage is of the first importance; but in the state, where success depends upon intellect, such a notion is not only fallacious, but fatal. Under the reign of Louis Philippe, any one who could write a decent leading article in a newspaper immediately fancied himself versed in state policy, and felt persuaded that he had nothing to do but fly at high game in order to gratify his ambition. The success of M. Guizot and M. Thiers seemed a sufficient guarantee for the access to power of innumerable petty scribblers, who had neither the wisdom of the *doctrinaire* nor the eloquence of the historian.

M. GUIZOT.—M. Guizot, when he commenced his lectures on public history at the Sorbonne, appeared like a luminous meteor on the political horizon. The expression of his views of ancient literature, the energy and the dignity with which he explained to his admiring audience the philosophy and the religion of Rome and Greece, his ironical comparison of the present claimants to renown, were listened to with an enthusiasm which proved how thoroughly they were understood, how fully they were appreciated. It was a sight which can never be effaced from memory, when the crowded hall was filled with impatient students awaiting the presence of their much loved professor, who with difficulty threaded his way, amid immense applause, with a slow and solemn step, to the chair of the professor. He poured forth, at first slowly, in a continued flow of elegant language, eulogiums upon the great writers in his own language, and then, with an impetuosity that seemed to convey an electric impetus around, his face, at first sombre and inexpressive, lighted up with supernatural animation; and as he gazed around, he inspired each of his auditors with the conviction that he was listening to a being of a superior order.

In the Assembly, M. Guizot spoke in a different style from what he did at the Sorbonne; and it was somewhat difficult to define the emotion that predominated in him: no sense either of triumph or of defeat was apparent. Cold, sombre, and meditative, he spoke with authority; and it was only at rare intervals that any great animation was visible in his countenance. It is no discredit to those statesmen that they earned their livelihood by writing for the newspapers; indeed, M. Guizot, aided by Madame Guizot, derived his subsistence for a long time from his literary labour. But they were the innocent cause of much mischief; for many a scribe who contributed a few lines to some journal anticipated the time when he might become Prime Minister of France.

M. Thiers.—It was in the Legislative Assembly that M. Thiers appeared to most advantage; but neither his matter nor his manner awoke the same feeling as those of his great competitor for power. An acute reasoner and an eloquent declaimer, though his voice is naturally harsh and shrill, his gestures are striking and animated, and he fixed the attention even of his political opponents. He marshalled his arguments with incredible skill, and brought out the caprices of his thought with energy and with decision. His countenance became animated as he spoke; and though his brilliant intelligence is tinged by a sarcastic expression not always befitting, his physiognomy is pleasing and occasionally winning. Upon the British Ambassador, Lord Normanby, he seemed to produce a great effect; for the noble Lord, who generally slumbered gently through the debate in the diplomatic *loge,* always woke up when M. Thiers commenced one of those brilliant attacks upon the administration, which at length unseated his powerful rival.

Lamartine.—There was a period when much was expected from Lamartine. Certainly no one did more for the safety of Paris than he did during the first days of the revolution of 1848; but there was too much poetry in his head for a statesman. He was too much absorbed in himself to think of his friends; the consequence was, that he never made up a party to support him: indeed he always stood aloof from any associations. His soirees on Saturday evenings in the Rue de l'Université were most agreeable, but were only social: every one sought access to them. They were presided over by Madame Lamartine, a highly-accomplished Englishwoman, daughter of Colonel Birch of Norfolk. She was an amateur artist, and took great delight in sculpture; a bust of her husband from her chisel is one of the best likenesses we have of Lamartine. At his reunions were to be seen the principal literary and political persons of the day, and all the distinguished artists; but amongst them were no attached friends. Many persons expected that he would be elected the first President of the Republic; and this most probably would have been the case, had not Louis Napoleon presented himself, for Lamartine was preferred to Cavaignac. The poet foresaw that the name of Bonaparte would carry everything before it, and was one of those who opposed the admission into France of all who belonged to that family.

Prince Louis Napoleon.—Great was the eagerness of every one to know the opinion that had been formed in England of the Prince Louis Napoleon. It was only known that he was looked on there as a perfect gentleman; but nobody could understand why he should have had himself sworn in as a special constable on the occasion of the Chartist demonstration of the 10th of April, and various were the reasons assigned.

His first speech in the Legislative Assembly was expected to be an explanation of his policy; it was, however, brief and modest. The election of the Prince as President of the Republic may be considered as a national triumph, as it certainly proved a national benefit; for he immediately took steps to organise a competent ministry, and commenced carrying into effect the improvements that his mind had long been engaged in studying. His speeches, his addresses, gave evidence of a vigorous intelligence, and he now and then astonished his ministers by the boldness of his language. This was the case at the inauguration of the railroad at Dijon, on which occasion he delivered an address, which M. Leon Faucher, his then Prime Minister, took care to alter before he gave it publicity. The Prince had occasion sometimes to change his ministry, according as circumstances permitted, but his selections uniformly gave satisfaction to the country. The station of Minister of Finance was filled for the most part by M. Achille Fould, who, amid all the varied changes in the political world, has maintained a well-deserved popularity, whilst his attachment to the Emperor has been both political and personal.

THE COUP D'ÉTAT.—The simple narrative of an unprejudiced individual who has witnessed some of the scenes of that extraordinary event, the *coup d'état* of 2d December 1851, and who has had opportunities of forming a judgment for himself of many of the circumstances attendant upon it, will, I am persuaded, be received with indulgence as a contribution of facts, for the accuracy of which I am able to vouch from my personal knowledge.

As a boy I read with infinite delight the volumes that described one of the most remarkable revolutions that history has recorded, and which was effected almost entirely by two daring women. The Empress Catherine of Russia and the Princess Dashkoff in a single night hurled from his throne the despotic autocrat of all the Russias; when his bold and ambitious wife seized his crown, and ruled the empire with uninterrupted power.

I have perused with attention most of the works that have contained a narrative of the events during the memorable days of December 1851, and I am persuaded that the public mind in England has been influenced by accounts written by persons who, not having witnessed them, or been acquainted with the state of society in Paris, have drawn inferences not justified by the actual position of affairs at that eventful period. One work, written by a man of high literary talent, appears to have been brought out for the express purpose of calumniating the Emperor and his ministers. How fallacious are some of the contributions to the history of that time may be inferred from the fact that they affect to narrate what was passing within the walls of the palace of the Elysée whilst the conflict was going on in the streets of Paris; even so minutely, as to describe the attitude and sayings of the individual who, at the same time, is spoken of as solitary, and brooding by himself over the probable issue of the struggles.

State of Public Feeling in Paris.—Every thinking person in Paris, towards the close of the year 1851, anticipated, with considerable apprehension, that early in the ensuing spring a great change must take place in the government of the country. The constitution, which had been proclaimed with apparent enthusiasm in the year 1848, appeared likely to produce anarchy and confusion; for a new President and an Assembly had to be elected, and whatever claims the individual who had once acted as head of the state might have upon the country, he was, according to the constitution, ineligible again to fill that high position. There was every reason to fear that the Red Republicans would make a desperate effort to gain power, even should the streets of Paris again be deluged with blood; indeed, the language of some of their adherents boldly proclaimed that liberty could only be secured by means of the guillotine. In effect, a struggle for power had commenced between the Prince-President and the representatives of the people. The Assembly had refused to grant to the chief of the state the funds necessary to defray the expenses attendant upon his position; it manifested distrust of his ministers, and jealousy of his popularity with the army, of which Changarnier had the command; and so mean were the devices resorted to to annoy Louis Napoleon, that he was compelled to wear at reviews the uniform of a general of the National Guard. A decided opposition was being organised against his re-election; and there is no doubt that his personal liberty was menaced by his opponents, and that, had not the *coup d'état* taken place, his career would have terminated in the fortress of

Vincennes. The candidature of the Prince de Joinville for the Presidency of 1852, which was very popular in France, even among the Liberal party, and seemed likely to be successful, disquieted the Bonapartists; and the violent and insolent language of General Changarnier aroused Louis Napoleon to the conviction that the time for action had arrived. It was the general opinion that a crisis was rapidly approaching, and only the President had the skill and courage to place himself at the head of the movement, and act decisively.

THE PRINCE-PRESIDENT.—The Prince-President naturally looked to that great source of power in all governments, the army, as his strongest support; as military discipline secures prompt and efficient action at the bidding of one directing mind. The army, having already been disgusted by the interference of the Legislative body, felt humiliated by the Republicans, and hailed with delight the expected advent of a bold leader. At the end of November the principal military authorities met at the house of General Magnan, and unanimously resolved to co-operate in any measures necessary to secure the tranquillity of Paris, and establish a firm and resolute government. The whole army being stationed in the vicinity of the metropolis, was prepared for some decisive movement; and although its precise nature was not understood, yet there was a determination to obey any orders emanating from the military authorities, whatever might be the consequence.

Relying on the support that he was thus to receive, the Prince-President announced to some of his faithful followers that the time had at length arrived when it was necessary for the welfare of the country, as well as for his own preservation, that measures should be adopted to dismiss the Assembly, and to give into his own hands the reins of government. Upon every occasion Louis Napoleon has secured to himself many attached adherents and friends, who have devotedly followed his fortunes on desperate occasions, and have not failed him in adversity. Such fidelity and devotion, while it reflects honour on them, also indicates rare qualities in the Prince, who exercises so powerful an influence over his adherents. His winning, unaffected manners, his calm self-possession, the deliberation and coolness of his judgment, and his firm conviction of his ultimate success, which have borne Louis Napoleon through difficulties apparently insurmountable, have never failed to impress all who have been admitted to his intimacy. He has also obtained the well-merited reputation of never having alienated or forgotten a friend.

M. de Morny.—The friend who stood forward on this occasion, and in whom the President felt that he could place the utmost reliance, was M. de Morny, a man of firm determination and keen intellect, who was well acquainted with the state of political feeling in France, and was friendly with some of the most distinguished men of the day. He entered into the plan proposed with a full conviction that he was acting the part of a good citizen, and an attached friend, and zealously devoted himself to the cause of the Prince; indeed, much of its success must be attributed to his admirable arrangements. Throughout he exhibited that calm but energetic and indomitable spirit essential on great occasions. He was at the Opera Comique on the very night when the storm was to burst forth; but nothing in his manner or appearance betrayed that his mind was absent from the dramatic scene.

The following anecdote is related of him, of the truth of which there can be no doubt. Being seated beside a lady of high rank, she asked him if the rumour in circulation was true, that it was intended to sweep out the Legislative Assembly; the prompt reply of the future Minister of the Interior was, "I trust that I shall be near the handle of the broom that is to produce this effect." His tact, his temper, and his moderation may be judged of by the telegraphic despatches which passed, during the tumult of the day, between himself and the Minister of Police. The celebrated Dr Veron occupied himself for some time in copying these messages as they were transmitted; and the experienced editor of the *Constitutionnel* has enabled the public to judge how rapidly M. de Morny entered into the ideas of the Minister of Police, and how cautiously yet vigorously he answered the somewhat hurried and imprudent communications that he received.

Major (now General) Fleury, a most gallant officer who had greatly distinguished himself in Africa, was another individual upon whose remarkable abilities the Prince had the strongest reliance; to these personal friends were added M. de Maupas, who had, in the exercise of his high authority as Préfet at Bordeaux, shewn qualifications which entitled him to be intrusted with the important office of Minister of Police. Two distinguished men of high rank in the army represented the military element; General (afterwards Marshal) St Arnaud accepted the onerous position of Minister of War, and General (now Marshal) Magnan was appointed to the command of the army at Paris.

THE NIGHT OF DECEMBER 1.—On the evening of the 1st of December, a gay and fashionable assembly congregated at the palace of the Elysée; all was gaiety and animation as usual; it was a *fête* of social life, into which care never seemed to enter: to-morrow seemed never dreamt of. The Prince joined the lively throng; no trace of care was upon his brow: he was apparently bent only on making happy the friends by whom he was surrounded; and, with his usual affability and kindness, he spoke to several of those who were for the first time present, giving to all a hearty welcome. At eleven o'clock the party broke up, and the visitors departed.

Then the Prince, with his faithful friend and secretary M. Mocquard, the Comte de Morny, M. de Maupas, and General St Arnaud, entered the private cabinet of the President, to arrange definitively the course of proceeding on the morrow. It was at this meeting that the final orders were issued to the various functionaries by whom the plan of operations were to be carried into effect. Everything had been well and maturely considered; even the minor details had been decided upon. To obtain possession of the Government press—to arrest some of those whose violent opposition was most to be dreaded—to prevent the meeting of the Legislative body—to distribute the different regiments in commanding position—to name a new ministry,—these were objects of vital importance, the failure of any one of which might endanger the success of the whole movement; and each of the members of this cabinet council had important duties to perform, which if neglected would produce irremediable confusion. Not one of these determined men failed in his purpose, and all acted in concert; each one felt that upon his own efficiency rested the lives and fortunes of his associates, and the complete success of the *coup*.

The first step taken by Louis Napoleon was to sign the dismissal of the existing ministry, the appointment of the new ministers to their respective offices, and to prepare those energetic proclamations which on the following morning were read with eager eyes by the astonished Parisians. An active and intelligent officer, Colonel Béville, had been selected to carry to the printing office the decrees that were to be disseminated; these consisted of appeals to the people, orders to the army, and the proclamation of the Préfet of Police. He took them to the national printing office, where he found that a hundred of the Garde Municipale had, with prudent foresight, been installed, with orders to obey his commands. The director, of course, complied with the injunctions of the Préfet of Police, and the printers were kept at work during the night under strict surveillance; and in the morning Paris was placarded with the President's decrees.

As soon as M. de Béville had left the room, M. de Morny, M. Maupas, and General St Arnaud repaired to their several posts, prepared to act simultaneously, and with the energy and boldness essential to secure success. The account given by Mr Kinglake of what occurred on the eve of the *coup d'état* is so far from being correct, that instead of manifesting the perturbation, nervousness, and apparent anxiety of mind so graphically described, the Prince quietly retired to rest, and simply gave orders that he should be awakened at five in the morning. He betrayed not the slightest emotion, and nothing transpired that could give the household the most remote intimation of what was about to occur: indeed, it is a well-known fact, that the domestics were as much surprised the following morning at learning that a revolution had taken place in Paris, as any other inhabitants of the city, for some of them actually sallied out to inquire of the servants of the English Embassy whether there was any truth in the reports that had reached them from without.

THE ARRESTS.—The Minister of Police, M. de Maupas, instantly summoned all the commissioners of the different arrondissements into his cabinet, and signed orders for the arrest of the leading members of the Legislative Assembly, which were to be carried into effect before the break of day. Strange to say, there was not a word of inquiry, not a sign of hesitation. These functionaries recognised at once the authority under which they were called upon to act, and performed their duties with marvellous promptitude and with unfailing efficiency. The prisons of Paris received the men who the day before were the legislators and governors of France. Nor did the jailers hesitate (as was the case when Robespierre was overthrown) to open their gates for the reception of their late masters.

An anecdote is related, that General Changarnier was very nearly being made acquainted with the impending events. A young officer whose regiment was stationed at Courbevoie, had come up to Paris to pass the night; he was awoke by his servant, who told him that his presence was required immediately, as his regiment had been suddenly called out. The officer, surprised at this intelligence, and thinking that he ought to acquaint General Changarnier with this unusual order, went to the General's hotel; but finding that the porter was slow in opening the doors, he abandoned his intention and went to his quarters; whence he was obliged to accompany his regiment on the following day to overthrow the authority of General Changarnier and his friends. No delicacy was shewn in the manner of arresting the most distinguished men of the day; and the volume of M. Granier de Cassagnac, narrating what occurred in each case, has not met with general approbation: a little more consideration for men woke up in the dead of the night to be thrown into prison, would have better become that injudicious writer.

M. de Morny, after playing at whist at the Jockey Club with Colonel Feray and Count Daru, went to the hotel of the Minister of the Interior at five in the morning, and found the actual possessor of the office enjoying a peaceful slumber, from which he was speedily awakened to find himself superseded. The Chamber of Deputies was dissolved; some of the members in vain attempted to assemble and form a house, but they were removed and imprisoned for the day in the barracks on the Quai d'Orsay, whilst others were distributed amongst the neighbouring forts. Cromwell, when he drove the members out of the House of Commons, and the first Napoleon, when he boldly turned the representatives of the people out of their chamber at St Cloud, could not have acted with more energy and decision than was shewn on this occasion; and apparently under the sanction of the law, for the ministers had their instructions direct from the President of the Republic, who, as the executive power, was invested with the authority of arrest and imprisonment. All the different *employés* of Government, therefore, whether civil or military, carried out the commands they received without a moment's hesitation, coming as they did from the quarter which they were accustomed to regard as being responsible for what they did. In short, everything worked well, and the Government was soon in the hands of those who had so adroitly planned and so boldly carried out the *coup d'état.*

It now remained to keep the people tranquil, and to preserve the public peace from those daring Republicans, who would be certain to take advantage of any movement that might afford them an opportunity of seizing power, and to whom any amount of bloodshed would be considered of little consequence, so that their ends could be obtained.

PARIS ON DECEMBER 2.—Upon the 2d of December, totally unsuspicious of what was going forward, I left my house, and was somewhat surprised to witness great agitation amongst the people in the streets, who, for the most part, seemed anxious to return to their homes. I saw various groups reading placards of a large size upon the walls of every street, that had evidently been posted up by order of Government, as they were printed on white paper; for since the revolution of 1848, all private announcements have, by order of the police, been printed upon coloured paper. Knowing that at the mayoralty of my arrondissement every authentic document would appear on the *façade*, I hastened thither; besides, I was anxious to know what was said by the street politicians, who are in the habit of daily visiting the public office, outside which the *Moniteur* is daily affixed.

I found two proclamations attracting the eager attention of the readers: one was a *plebiscité*, countersigned De Morny, decreeing that votes should be taken at the different mayoralties for or against the maintenance of the power of Louis Napoleon; the other emanated from the Préfet du Police, demanding the maintenance of order, and recommending people to remain at home. Little was said by the readers; but in the group I espied a well-known Figaro of the neighbourhood, who whilst shaving his customers usually launched out into politics. He was a stanch Bonapartist, for his father, a soldier, had been raised to the rank of sergeant in consequence of a brave but ineffectual attempt to rescue Prince Poniatowski from a watery grave at the battle of

Leipsic. I determined to submit my chin to the operation of this worthy during the afternoon, feeling sure that I should hear information from him as to what was the general opinion of his customers. In the meantime I strolled into the Faubourg St Honoré, where a squadron of the 12th Regiment of Dragoons was stationed before the British Embassy, another being drawn up in front of the palace of the Elysée, whilst there was a third doing duty at the garden gate. A few individuals stood gazing on the unusual military display; but not a word was uttered, and they soon passed on. Now and then a carriage drove up to the gate, and after a scrutiny from the porter, was admitted or rolled away. So far as I could learn, no demonstration of any kind was made that day at the fashionable end of the town; but it was said that the Republicans were to have, at ten o'clock at night, meetings to take into consideration the incidents of the day; and that in the Faubourg St Antoine, the Barrière du Trône, and the Faubourg du Temple, cries had been heard of "Vive la République sociale!" and "À bas le Prétendant!"

After reconnoitring the principal streets, and seeing nothing remarkable, beyond the anxiety and curiosity written upon the faces of most persons, and witnessing, what is not unusual in the streets of Paris, the marching by of several regiments evidently in high glee, I adjourned to the barber's, and seated myself in his chair. He was in a state of great excitement, and expatiating on the many virtues of Prince Louis Napoleon, with which he had become acquainted from having on two occasions dressed the hair of the chambermaid whose duty it was to lay the fire over-night in the cabinet of the President, which he himself generally lighted at an early hour in the morning. The excellent *soubrette* could never speak in sufficiently high terms of the gentleness and amiable temper of her master, and the worthy barber had caught the infection. Deriving his information from her as to the Prince's domestic virtues, and inheriting his father's admiration of the great Napoleon, he launched out in no measured terms against all those who opposed the re-election of the President, though his animosity to the Republicans was somewhat restrained by the presence of two doubtful-looking statesmen in blouses, who now and then interrupted him, by expressing their faith in General Changarnier. My eloquent friend, however, soon resumed his discourse, anathematising M. Thiers as having obliged King Louis Philippe to resign, that he himself might become Prime Minister to the Duchess of Orleans, and hurling strong language against M. Emile Girardin, for abetting Prince Napoleon, the cousin of Prince Louis, in his views of succeeding to the Presidentship: he had heard some cries in the street of "Vive l'Empereur!" from the military, and they had delighted him. Some of the surrounding persons, waiting to have their beards trimmed, differed from the knight of the brush; doubts were expressed of the talent of the Prince-President, and there was evidently a Republican tendency springing up; but the announcement that the Prince, attended by a numerous staff, was passing by, put a stop to the conversation; away every one rushed out to see the passing show, and upon their return there was a universal opinion expressed, that the Prince-President looked like a noble soldier, and "every inch a king:" his gallant bearing had evidently produced a strong impression upon the spectators, the majority of whom from that moment were evidently in favour of the changes that had taken place.

LOUIS NAPOLEON AT THE ELYSÉE.—It has been asserted that the Prince-President remained in his cabinet, during these eventful days, solitary and gloomy, and, like the Roman emperor at Capreæ, solely occupied in issuing his edicts for the destruction of his opponents. This story originally emanated from an author more distinguished for the brilliancy of his imagination than for the soberness of his judgment, or the accuracy of his knowledge; and who was conspicuous for his political malevolence, and the virulence of his speeches in the Legislative Assembly. He has been followed by some who, whilst they claim to write history, have no hesitation in copying the errors and exaggerations of others; but it can safely be asserted that, so far from Prince Louis Napoleon being left to himself, the Princesse Mathilde remained with him the greater part of the day; King Jerome and most of the new ministers were admitted, and the Elysée was not closed to any visitors who had a right to present themselves to the President. Those who were received, found him calm, collected, and urbane as usual; and as notes and messages were placed in his hands, he received them with coolness, and quietly read their contents; but never, by his countenance, his gestures, or his words, could the effect or import of these communications be inferred. He addressed all with his customary affability and kindness, and conversed freely upon various topics. The Emperor, it is true, does not possess that volubility for which Frenchmen are remarkable; he thinks and weighs his words before he speaks, and what he says is concise and to the point: his manner is quiet and reticent, like that of a grave and thoughtful man; but this quietude is amply made up for by the flattering attention which he gives to the words of all with whom he speaks: nothing escapes him; he listens intelligently to all that is said, and his replies and observations evince a wish not to express his own opinion, but to learn that of others; and he never fails to appreciate at their due the value of the views and opinions brought before him. Upon these eventful days the Prince maintained his usual equanimity, and was not more grave and silent than usual; he never for an instant flinched from possible danger; he was always prepared to meet it; indeed, the man who had so boldly advanced into his enemy's country at Strasbourg and at Boulogne, was not likely to be daunted or quailed when so much was already accomplished; and his followers had seen enough of his conduct in such emergencies, to be satisfied of his presence of mind and personal courage.

M. de Persigny, whose attachment to the Emperor is such that he would at any moment lay down his life for him and for his dynasty, was constantly at the Elysée; for to him had been intrusted the task of effecting an honourable retreat, in case of an adverse turn of circumstances. His duty it would have been, had the day gone against the President, to have collected the household, and to have conducted the Prince, with all the troops that were faithful, to the palace of the Tuileries, where the active leaders were determined to make a last stand, and succeed, or perish with arms in their hands. This was the only alternative proposed; no preparations had been made for flight; no horses and carriages kept ready, no money had been sent to foreign countries, and nothing had been packed up to be carried off at a moment's notice. There was a firm resolve that death or victory was to be the result of this great enterprise.

In the course of the first day, I paid a visit to an old comrade, that distinguished officer Sir de Lacy Evans, who had just come to Paris, and was residing in the Place de la Madeleine; the conversation naturally turned on the events passing before our eyes, and the General expressed much satisfaction at the apparent promptitude with which the affair had been carried out; for we believed that public tranquillity had not been disturbed. He observed that the enemies of the Prince-President had brought the whole thing upon themselves, by their shameful treatment of the chief of the state; adding, that he felt persuaded that if Louis Napoleon would give the people a liberal constitution, which should include the freedom of the press, he would prove himself a greater man than his uncle.

I had been told that a column of the National Guard had marched with the infantry, but I found that this was not the case; in fact the utmost care had been taken not to call out the National Guard, for it was well known that in some of the regiments there were Republicans, who might be induced to leave their brethren and join the insurgents, if they were disposed to raise barricades. The consequence was that everything depended upon the regular troops.

Reception of the Prince-President.—When the Prince, attended by a numerous staff, accompanied by the ex-King Jerome and by Count Flahault, rode through the streets, he exhibited that bravery which has never deserted him in the hour of danger; notwithstanding the calumnies of his traducers, who choose to assert that he is deficient in personal courage and nerve. He was remarkably well received by the army, and shouts of "Vive le Prince!" were heard from every regiment, as he cantered along the Champs Elysées. The people of Paris are never demonstrative in their reception of their monarchs; even the ordinary token of respect to royalty, the lifting of the hat, is rare, and on this occasion there was no observable departure from the usual habit. The Prince-President returned at an early hour to the Elysée, where M. de Persigny received him with the intelligence that all the steps hitherto taken were successful, and that the military were fully prepared to fulfil the orders of their superiors; indeed, so obedient were the sentries to the commands which had been given, that when the President, preparing to leave the garden of the palace, presented himself at the gate, the advanced guard of the 12th Regiment, then on duty, would not allow him to pass without giving the countersign. The orderly officers and the aides-de-camp gave proofs of their courage, zeal, and devotion. At one moment false reports were rife, that some of the regiments exhibited an unwillingness to act; General Rollin was summoned to express his opinion, and explain the state of affairs; he found the Prince firm and resolved, and prepared to take upon himself any personal responsibility for any steps that might be necessary. In short, every one who approached the Prince—and these were many—were struck with admiration at his dignified equanimity and self-possession.

Alarm of the Parisians.—The news of the imprisonment of so many persons of great political importance, spread like wildfire throughout the whole of Paris, whilst the suddenness and the boldness of their arrest astonished and struck terror into the minds of many. Much sympathy was felt for them individually; and the horrors of the great French Revolution, the massacres in the prisons, the slaughter of priests, the banishment to Cayenne, rose up before the affrighted imaginations of the friends and relations of those who had been imprisoned. In the *cafés* a profound silence was observed; all communication from man to man seemed suddenly to have ceased; and anxiety was depicted on every countenance. The *salons* of the gay world were necessarily closed, as few dared to venture forth in the evening, no one knowing the extent of the danger that might be incurred. Were there to be Roman proscriptions? Was the guillotine to be erected once again on the Place de la Concorde? Lists of the prisoners (which of course abounded with errors) were eagerly circulated, and surmises were made as to their probable fate. It must be acknowledged that these alarms were natural, for the real disposition of the Prince was not known, otherwise there would have been less uneasiness, as was evinced by the fact that the gentlest treatment had been recommended, and that not a single individual arrested received the slightest insult or injury. Indeed, as soon as quietness was re-established, and the influence of the members of the Assembly could no longer be of consequence, every one was liberated; and not a person was in any way interfered with who was willing to submit to the new state of things. Some who menaced the newly-established government, were necessarily exiled for a short period, to prevent their entering upon schemes which could be only injurious to society and themselves. But as soon as possible a complete amnesty was offered; and those who announced their intention to remain quiet were at once allowed to return to their homes. Those who were taken with arms in their hands, and had proclaimed the Republic, were handed over for trial to the established tribunals, and only those were removed from the country whose character as disturbers of society had been previously acknowledged. In the conduct of the new government throughout, there was nothing that could justify the attacks that had been made, and the assertion that cruelties were inflicted upon innocent and harmless persons. In all great emergencies there are circumstances which, in the more peaceful states of society, would be highly reprehensible; the moment called for the establishment of a Dictator: "Nequid respublica detrimenti caperet." Democracy, Socialism, Red-Republicanism were to be combated, and success attended the grand attempt. Property and intelligence have been rendered secure; the boldness and energy of one man have crushed dangers to society which were seen to be fast approaching, and which, if not arrested, would have produced anarchy and confusion, and destroyed the peace and prosperity of the nation. The measures that the Prince-President was compelled to take, naturally excited the wrath of the very men who would have overthrown him; and every means were resorted to, by a small knot of aggrieved persons, to excite the indignation of the people at the recital of the misfortunes that fell upon those who exposed themselves to peril on an eventful day. Much was necessarily done in the defence of order which those who live where tranquillity has been for centuries established cannot fully comprehend; and the sympathy that is felt for the weak and suffering, has been called into activity by some who are incapable of judging fairly of the circumstances.

THE LEGISLATIVE ASSEMBLY.—But whatever sympathy may have been felt for individuals, none whatever was expressed or shewn for the body to which they belonged. The abrupt dismissal of the Legislative Assembly was not regretted by any one; on the contrary, it was considered as a benefit to the country. The Assembly had never gained or deserved the confidence of the people, and not one of its acts could be cited that was worthy of a great nation.

Even the Provisional Government, during its short and feverish existence, had shewn some proofs of its desire to benefit society; it had abrogated the laws that punished political offences with death; it had ameliorated the hardships of the debtor; carried out some excellent improvements in the direction of railways, and had boldly met the financial exigencies by additional taxation, whilst it had removed the vexatious *octroi.* But the Legislative Assembly seemed to take a delight in repealing every statute that had given satisfaction to the nation; its aim appeared to be to return to the legislation of MM. Molé, Guizot, and Thiers; and it was remarkable for its ingratitude to any man who had done the state service. M. Lamartine, to whom Paris was so much indebted, whose eloquence had controlled the fierce democracy when the mob would have supplanted the tricolor by the red flag at the Hôtel de Ville, could scarcely command attention; nothing that he said was listened to. Cabals against General Cavaignac, the man to whom they were indebted for their existence, prevented his influence having due weight, and he was forsaken as soon as he ceased to be useful. Their presidents were utterly disregarded; the high-minded and finished gentleman, Armand Marrast, could not control the debates; M. Dupin was only regarded by them as a clever jester, whose caustic wit and epigrammatic reproofs served to amuse; his judicious admonitions and calls to order were unheeded, and the Assembly was too often the scene of virulent dispute and indecent violence. The tumult and clamour attending the appearance of any unpopular member in the tribune were disgraceful. When Victor Hugo attempted to speak, bursts of laughter followed some striking remarks which were not in accordance with the sentiments of the Assembly; the taunts and marks of ridicule lashed the speaker into a fury, and the more vehement his speech and gestures, the more his auditors derided him. There were many men of great ability in the Assembly who were esteemed by the country at large, but general opinion was not in favour of the body, and its disorganisation was regarded with much the same indifference as was the breaking up of the Rump Parliament by Oliver Cromwell; the announcement of its dissolution, therefore, was favourably received. There had been so many changes in the ministry, that people hardly knew who filled the respective offices; Leon Faucher was almost the only one who enjoyed public confidence, and even he was regarded by a large party with suspicion, for they beheld in him only a warming-pan for the advent to office of M. Thiers, who was supposed to be ready to take advantage of any change, and offer himself as candidate for the Presidency of the Republic. Rumours widely circulated that a *coup d'état* was preparing on the part of the Assembly, and many of its acts seemed to support this idea: such as the attempt to place under the authority of the Assembly a large military guard, and the defiant and menacing language of General Changarnier, then in command of the army. The apprehensions of the people were constantly aroused, and conflicts were daily expected; foreign statesmen looked with anxiety at what was passing, and the alarm upon the Continent was increased by the expedition to Rome; for, however much such a check upon the policy of Austria might be necessary, French interference with the Republican party in Italy was looked upon with suspicion. In fact, the National Assembly had lost the respect and confidence of the nation, and no one was anxious to see it reassemble. The protests and appeals to the people, made by some few members on the morning of the 2d of December, were received with apathy, and elicited no exhibition of feeling in their behalf; for, when at the Mairie arrests took place, no rescue was dreamt of; the spectators gazed on quietly, and were perfectly indifferent to the consequences.

THE 3D AND 4TH OF DECEMBER.—Slight barricades were formed in some of the streets, but the people took little interest in these manifestations on the first day; on the 3d of December, however, greater resistance was offered. But evidently M. de Maupas received exaggerated reports from his *employés*, which he somewhat hastily communicated to the Minister of the Interior; and these, unfortunately, led to the decisive and energetic course taken on the melancholy 4th of December. M. de Maupas, unaccustomed to the amplifications of police agents, was alarmed by false reports; he actually communicated a telegram announcing that the Prince de Joinville had disembarked at Cherbourg, and that other Princes of the house of Orleans had arrived at different parts of France. He also believed that the same opponents were in the field as those who had fought against Cavaignac, and that they were fighting at the barricades with determination; that Ledru Rollin, and a whole army of Red Republicans, had reached Paris from Rouen; in short, upon reading carefully the telegraphic despatches, the only conclusion that can be arrived at is, that the fears of M. de Maupas, and not the orders issued from the Elysée, were the principal cause of the fatal 4th of December.

On Thursday, at a quarter past one, M. de Maupas, as Préfet of Police, transmitted a telegram to the

Minister of the Interior, in which appears these words:—"Voilà le moment de frapper un coup décisif. Il faut le bruit et l'effet du canon, et il les faut tout de suite." The Minister of the Interior at this very time, when it has been asserted that the most sanguinary orders were issued, was exerting himself to see that the execution of all commands should be performed as inoffensively as possible:—"N'arrêtons pas légèrement." "Cet ordre sera exécuté avec beaucoup de politesse." "Faites fermer avec douceur la réunion." "Je ne veux pas que vos agents arrêtent légèrement." Such words, combined with other proofs, shew that there was no intention on the part of the adherents of the Prince to act with brutal force. The poor Préfet of Police seems, indeed, to have lost his head. Among other of his despatches I find the following:—"It is said that the 2d Dragoons (the very regiment that was guarding the Elysée) has arrived from St Germain, and that the Comte de Chambord is in its ranks as a private. I scarcely believe it." The only answer by M. de Morny was, "And I do not believe it." Even at the end of the fatal day, when everybody was regretting what had occurred, the frightened Minister of Police begs that the troops should guard him, that they should not be allowed to enter their barracks; and at half-past five on that 4th of December he announces new barricades, and states that fresh insurgents are coming up by the railroad. It is impossible to read the bulletins which passed on this occasion without arriving at the conclusion that M. de Morny, in obedience to the wishes of the Prince-President, acted with forbearance and lenity; that, had he listened to the fears of the Minister of Police, the occurrences would have been of a much more fearful character. Even when this zealous chief of an active department pointed out to M. de Morny where Victor Hugo was concealed, and wished to make an examination of the house, the answer was, "*Ne faites rien.*"

That the 4th of December was a melancholy day for France, and will long remain remembered by Europe, is not to be denied; but it is neither just nor honest to attribute the lamentable events which then occurred to cold-heartedness on the part of Louis Napoleon. No man ever more deeply deplored them; and where the opportunity offered, he gave what indemnity he could to the families of those who had suffered. There are young persons who lost their parents on that day who have been educated at his expense, the cost being defrayed out of his private purse; and I know myself one instance in which the children have had a regular quarterly stipend paid to them, from their infancy, and which is continued, without interruption or diminution, to this day.

The first impression made upon the minds of people in England as to what occurred on the 4th of December, was the result of a letter which appeared in the *Times*, from an officer of the British army, who, from a window on the Boulevard Montmartre, was a personal witness of the scene that took place in the street beneath him, where many persons fell victims to the fire of the soldiery. The infantry, quartered in sub-divisions, suddenly fired, not only upon the men, women, and children in the footpath, but at the windows above them, and with sad results: volley succeeded to volley, and it was evident that a panic had taken possession of the soldiery. Their officers had given no commands; for, as Captain Jesse observes, they were quietly smoking their cigars when the firing began.

From the reports of the agents of the Minister of Police in the quarter of St Denis, firing from the windows took place at the commencement of the military impulse. "*Des maisons sont déjà occupées par l'émeute; on a tiré des fenêtres,*" were the words transmitted from the office of the Minister of Police. It was this alarm that produced the fatal consequences. The windows of the houses had on former occasions been filled by insurgents who fired upon the troops, when the soldiers suffered so severely as to be under the necessity of watching for concealed foes, and had been obliged to rush into a house with the hope of dragging forth their enemies. In 1848, in the Rue Castiglione, two soldiers were killed by shots from the third story of a house, whilst a lady was quietly standing on the balcony above. The soldiery, too, remember that, in the days of Louis Philippe, from a window of a house upon one of the Boulevards, not very far from the spot where Captain Jesse was standing, a deadly volley was discharged, by which many military were killed; amongst them Marshal Mortier, as brave a soldier as ever drew a sword for his country. It is not to be denied that considerable irritation existed amongst the military, from the recollection of what had occurred during the Revolution in 1848, when they were most shamefully treated;—they recollected the carnage and the burning alive of the brave men in the guard-house before the Palais-Royal; they bore in mind the treachery which some of their comrades experienced in the Champs Elysées; and there existed amongst them a strong feeling against the Parisians generally. The firing of the soldiers at the house of M. Sallandrouze, near which was Captain Jesse's apartment, was occasioned by some persons standing on the steps cheering at what they supposed was the employment of blank cartridge by the troops.

What the Author Saw.—I happened on that day to pay a visit, in company with my friend Mr Paget of the British Embassy, to my banker in the Rue Basse du Rampart: Mr Charles Lafitte then gave us to understand that orders had been given to the military to act with great moderation; but if there existed the slightest disposition to riot, they were to "take the bull by the horns," and to destroy all barricades with cannon. During our short interview the bugles were heard close at hand, the windows were opened, and we took up a position on the balcony, whence we saw marching, in good military order and at double quick time, the Chasseurs of Vincennes. M. Lafitte, without anticipating what was about to occur, good-naturedly said, "If you wish to see the fun, you had better follow the troops; for I am confident, from the information I have this moment received, that they are bent on mischief."

Mr Paget and I then bent our steps towards the Rue Richelieu, where the rattling of musketry was distinctly heard. My friend left for the British Embassy, saying, that as a diplomatist, his place was in the Faubourg St Honoré and not upon the Boulevards. Immediately afterwards a brigade of Lancers, commanded by Colonels Feray and Rochefort, arrived opposite the spot where I had placed myself, at the angle of the Rue Grange Batelière and the Boulevards. A considerable crowd had there collected; and such was their hostile attitude, and so loud their vociferations, that I was convinced the Lancers would not long remain inactive, especially if the slightest insult was offered them. From amongst these persons thus collected came a pistol ball with a loud detonation, and a soldier was wounded. Col. Rochefort immediately charged at the head of his regiment; the consequence was that several of the crowd were severely wounded, and a bad feeling sprang up amongst the soldiery. I thought it prudent to quit this scene and return to my home, which I reached with considerable difficulty.

Certainly, all that occurred was of a nature to excite uneasiness and alarm; but "that it was seen with frenzied horror by thousands of French men and women" is an absurd exaggeration. The upper classes of Paris were no doubt exceedingly angry and irritated, because during every émeute in the metropolis, the Boulevards on the Madeleine side of the Rue Richelieu always continued to be the resort of the *flâneur*, and had escaped the slaughter consequent on the erection of barricades; and they went there attracted by "the pomp and circumstance of war," and thought themselves safe; for they looked upon the soldiers as their national defenders against insurgents, and they were maddened at the idea of the slaughter of unarmed saunterers, who had gone out as it were under the shield of the military, to see what was going forward.

GROUNDLESS FABRICATIONS.—The occurrences of that day undoubtedly struck a terror into the hearts of the people of Paris which will never be obliterated, and they certainly have tended to affect the popularity of the Emperor Napoleon in the capital; more especially as his political adversaries have never failed to throw upon him the responsibility of events over which he had no control. So dishonest have been some of the writers who have furnished the public with their tales, that it has been stated that in the gardens of the Tuileries and the Luxembourg, military executions of prisoners took place in the dead of night! The overthrow of a pile of the chairs, which in winter are generally to be seen in the garden of the Tuileries, and the consequent alarm given by the sentry, was even magnified into an attack upon the palace and the consequent carnage of the assailants. As for the statement that platoons of soldiers performed the office of executioners in the night, it is a pure invention; and the rumour alleged to have been credited in Paris, that during the night of the 4th and 5th of December prisoners were shot in batches and thrown into pits, is an equally groundless fabrication. I never heard that such a falsehood was propagated, until I read this shameful insinuation in a volume which claims to be a contribution to history. As for the "nine kinds of slaughter" which the eccentric writer discovers that military men may unhesitatingly indulge in, I do not think that any of these have relation to the melancholy events of the 4th of December.

Those events are deeply to be deplored; but they arose out of accidental circumstances. No one has ever attempted to defend them; and they ought not to be exaggerated, either for the purpose of exciting the sympathy of nations, or for the sake of blackening political enemies. There was no wanton massacre of the people, as has been asserted; there were sad mistakes, and people ran into danger notwithstanding the warnings that were distributed everywhere—for placards were upon the walls in every direction, entreating every one to stay at home. There were insurgents, there were barricades, there was firing upon the soldiers; there was therefore a necessity for martial law to be enforced; but the

Emperor is not chargeable either with the wild excesses of the soldiery, or the credulity of the Minister of Police.

The Parisians, even at the height of their excitement, did not hold the Prince-President responsible for these deplorable consequences; neither had he the least apprehension of being the object of vindictive feelings. So far from entertaining any personal fear, his calm self-possession was never more conspicuous than during these eventful days. I will only mention one corroborative circumstance in proof of this.

On the fourth night after the *coup d'état*, my daughter and myself were present at a ball, given by the Duchess of Hamilton in honour of the Prince President, at the Hotel Bristol, Place Vendôme. At ten o'clock precisely, the President entered the ballroom, accompanied only by Count Bacciochi, when a quadrille was formed; the Prince dancing with the Duchess of Hamilton, Lady Poltimore and the Duke of Hamilton being the *vis-à-vis*. The second quadrille soon followed; when the Prince chose the Princess Mathilde as his partner, Lord Poltimore and Lady Cowley making the *vis-à-vis*.

The Prince appeared perfectly cool and collected; he conversed with a great many persons, but more particularly with Lord Cowley, who had only arrived in Paris that morning, to fill his post of British Ambassador. Lords Francis Gordon, Strangford, Halliburton, Ernest Bruce, with their wives, were present; together with many foreigners of distinction. The instant the clock struck twelve, Count Bacciochi, in a low whisper, said that the Prince's carriage was ready; whereupon the Duke of Hamilton, taking two wax-candles, conducted his imperial guest down-stairs, and handed him into his plain brougham. On the return of the Duke to the ball-room, he observed to several friends who had collected round him, "How extraordinary! There were neither military nor police in the court-yard of the hotel, to protect the President in case of danger." In fact, the Prince returned at midnight, without an escort, to the Elysée, in a one-horse brougham.

And this is the man whom Mr Kinglake, in his account of the *coup d'état*, has insinuated to be constantly occupied in guarding himself against attacks from assassination, and living in fear and trembling.

Let those who have been influenced by these calumnies, consider what have been the results of the *coup d'état* upon the position and prospects of

France. The nation enjoys greater prosperity and happiness, and its power and influence are stronger and more undisputed than ever in Europe; while the Emperor of the French holds a firm and lofty place amongst the monarchs of the world, in right of the wisdom with which he governs the people and develops the resources of the country.

THE END

CPSIA information can be obtained
at www.ICGtesting.com
Printed in the USA
LVHW112000050422
715401LV00006B/314

9 783752 587920